Drawn

What Reviewers Say About Carsen Taite's Work

Leading the Witness

"Every once in a while you need a good lawyer book, and when I say every once in a while I mean every time Carsen Taite writes a book. She is my go-to for a good crime/lawyer focused book. Every single time you get a fabulous read that will be hard to put down way past your bedtime."—*The Romantic Reader Blog*

"Carsen Taite is a sure bet."—*Jude in the Stars*

Practice Makes Perfect

"Absolutely brilliant! …I was hooked reading this story. It was intense, thrilling in that way legal matters get to the nitty gritty and instil tension between parties, fast paced, and laced with angst… Very slow burn romance, which not only excites me but makes me get so lost in the story."—*LESBIreviewed*

"…a fun start to a promising new series, with characters I enjoyed getting to know."—*Lesbian Review*

Pursuit of Happiness

"Taite has written a book that draws you in. It had us hooked from the first paragraph to the last. We thoroughly enjoyed this book and would unhesitatingly recommend it."—*Best Lesfic Reviews*

"…an entertaining read for anyone interested in American politics and its legal system."—*Lez Review Books*

Love's Verdict

"Well written, cleverly plotted, with a great balance between the slow change from dislike to attraction to love in the romance department while the high profile case works through its phases. The merging of the two plots is subtle and well-crafted seamlessly moving us forward on both fronts. The high profile murder is well played, as always with Ms Taite's courtroom dramas, and I liked the way it became a real life thriller as well as a legal case. Overall an excellent read, one of my favourites from this author."—*Lesbian Reading Room*

Outside the Law

"This is by far the best book of the series and Ms. Taite has saved the best for last. Each book features a romance and the main characters, Tanner Cohen and Sydney Braswell are well rounded, lovable and their chemistry is sizzling… The book found the perfect balance between romance and thriller with a surprising twist at the end. Very entertaining read. Overall, a very good end of this series. Recommended for both romance and thriller fans. 4.5 stars."—*Lez Review Books*

A More Perfect Union

"Readers looking for a mix of intrigue and romance set against a political backdrop will want to pick up Taite's latest novel." —*RT Book Reviews*

"…an excellent romantic suspense (which should be a surprise to no one, because that's exactly what Taite does!)… This is a pitch-perfect Carsen Taite story. Everything worked for me!"—*Lesbian Review*

Sidebar

"Sidebar is a love story with a refreshing twist. It's a mystery and a bit of a thriller, with an ethical dilemma and some subterfuge thrown in for good measure. The combination gives us a fast-paced read, which includes courtroom and personal drama, an appealing love story, and a more than satisfying ending." —*Lambda Literary Review*

"This book has it all, two fantastic lead characters, an interesting plot and that sizzling chemistry that great authors can make jump off the page. While all of Taite's books are fantastic, this one is on the next level. No critiques, no criticism, you only need to know one thing…this is a damn good book."—*Romantic Reader Blog*

Letter of the Law

"If you like romantic suspense novels, stories that involve the law, or anything to do with ranching, you're not going to want to miss this one."—*Lesbian Review*

Without Justice

"Another pretty awesome lesbian mystery thriller by Carsen Taite."—Danielle Kimerer, Librarian, Nevins Memorial Library (MA)

"All in all a fantastic novel… Unequivocally 5 Stars…"—*Les Rêveur*

Above the Law

"…readers who enjoyed the first installment will find this a worthy second act."—*Publishers Weekly*

Reasonable Doubt

"The story was a great ride! Mixing both dramatic moments with fast-paced action, along with heartfelt and gentle occurrences… Carsen Taite brought all of her own history as a criminal defense lawyer to the forefront of this novel in order to help tell the story. …Bravo to the author! A wonderful story all around. I will be adding Carsen Taite to my list of authors to watch for when new novels are released."—*FarNerdy Book Blog*

"The two main characters are well written and I was into them from the first minute they appeared. It's a modern thriller which takes place in the world right now."—*Lesfic Tumblr*

Lay Down the Law

"Recognized for the pithy realism of her characters and settings drawn from a Texas legal milieu, Taite pays homage to the prime-time soap opera *Dallas* in pairing a cartel-busting U.S. attorney, Peyton Davis, with a charity-minded oil heiress, Lily Gantry." —*Publishers Weekly*

"In typical suspense fashion, twists and turns abound as the two women collide within each other's spheres, eventually leading to the inevitable happy ending… This novel is recommended for general LGBT and mystery collections."—*GLBT Reviews: The ALA's Gay Lesbian Bisexual Transgender Round Table*

Courtship

"This is one really fine story. I felt as if I were right in the middle of a major political battle to get a relatively unknown woman appointed to the most important court position in the land. Levels upon levels plus twists and turns, including a passionate entanglement adding a spectacular underscore, as the lovers meld and re-meld multiple times. I would have to say this is a classic page-turner and I totally enjoyed the high-spirited elements that may always surround key political battles. Magnificent!" —*Rainbow Book Reviews*

Switchblade

"Dallas's intrepid female bounty hunter, Luca Bennett, is back in another adventure. Fantastic! Between her many friends and lovers, her interesting family, her fly by the seat of her pants lifestyle, and a whole host of detractors there is rarely a dull moment."—*Rainbow Book Reviews*

Rush

"A simply beautiful interplay of police procedural magic, murder, FBI presence, misguided protective cover-ups, and a superheated love affair…a Gold Star from me and major encouragement for all readers to dive right in and consume this story with gusto!" —*Rainbow Book Reviews*

Battle Axe

"Taite breathes life into her characters with elemental finesse… A great read, told in the vein of a good old detective-type novel filled with criminal elements, thugs, and mobsters that will entertain and amuse."—*Lambda Literary*

Slingshot

"The mean streets of lesbian literature finally have the hard boiled bounty hunter they deserve. It's a slingshot of a ride, bad guys and hot women rolled into one page turning package. I'm looking forward to Luca Bennett's next adventure."—J. M. Redmann, author of the Micky Knight mystery series

Nothing but the Truth

"As a criminal defense attorney in Dallas, Texas, Carsen Taite knows her way around the court house. …*Nothing But the Truth* is an enjoyable mystery with some hot romance thrown in."—*Just About Write*

It Should be a Crime—*Lammy Finalist*

"This [*It Should be a Crime*] is just Taite's second novel…, but it's as if she has bookshelves full of bestsellers under her belt. In fact, she manages to make the courtroom more exciting than Judge Judy bursting into flames while delivering a verdict. Like this book, that's something we'd pay to see."—*Gay List Daily*

By the Author

Truelesbianlove.com

It Should be a Crime

Do Not Disturb

Nothing but the Truth

The Best Defense

Beyond Innocence

Rush

Courtship

Reasonable Doubt

Without Justice

Sidebar

A More Perfect Union

Love's Verdict

Pursuit of Happiness

Leading the Witness

Drawn

The Luca Bennett Mystery Series:

Slingshot

Battle Axe

Switchblade

Bow and Arrow (novella in Girls with Guns)

Lone Star Law Series:

Lay Down the Law

Above the Law

Letter of the Law

Outside the Law

Legal Affairs Romances:

Practice Makes Perfect

Drawn

by

Carsen Taite

2020

DRAWN

ISBN 13: 978-1-63555-644-5

This Trade Paperback Original Is Published By
Bold Strokes Books, Inc.
P.O. Box 249
Valley Falls, NY 12185

First Edition: June 2020

Credits
Editor: Cindy Cresap
Production Design: Susan Ramundo
Cover Design By Tammy Seidick

Acknowledgments

After setting my last couple of books in Austin, Texas, (a place I love), I decided to return to another place I love, the city I call home. Dallas aka Big D's motto is Big Things Happen Here and it's true. I'm lucky to reside in a city with a large and vibrant LGBTQ community where I can live openly and participate in lots of varied activities with my family of choice, including the Women with Pride book club now in its eleventh year. In addition to all the fun, queer stuff to do, Dallas is full of beautiful, fun, and sometimes funky landmarks. I was discussing these with my wife Lainey—the real artist in the family—when the idea for this book was born (she's the brainchild who came up with Riley Flynn). Thanks, L, for the ideas and the encouragement to live my dreams.

I also want to thank the usual suspects. Special shout outs to Rad and Sandy who run the most amazing publishing house on the planet—I'm proud to call Bold Strokes home. To my editor, Cindy Cresap, thanks for your tireless guidance to make me a better writer. Thanks to Tammy Seidick for another amazing cover. Ruth, you are the blurb muse and I'm forever grateful for your generous help. Sharon B., thanks for always being willing to talk about dead bodies. Your knowledge is invaluable, and any forensic errors are entirely my own.

The act of writing may be solitary, but every writer needs a supportive crew of pals to get them through the process and I have some of the best. Georgia, Melissa, Elle, and Paula—I raise a glass to each of you! And Paula, special thanks for lending your keen eyes to the first draft of this story and sticking with me to the very last word.

And most of all, thanks go to you, dear readers. Your support in the form of buying the book, writing reviews, and spreading the word is what makes it possible for me to earn a living doing the work I love. You're the best!

Dedication

To Lainey.
I’ve been drawn to you from the moment we met.

Chapter One

Riley stuck her brush in the small jar of water and stepped back to assess her creation. She'd spent the last half hour trying to perfect the background of the sunset against the mural on the side of Henry's Thrift Shop, but she couldn't seem to get the colors right and she couldn't help but think the trouble on her canvas was a reflection of the rest of her life lately.

"Still working?"

Riley turned toward the voice to see Mrs. Henry, the elderly owner of the store, the lone holdout of original businesses on this gentrified block of Deep Ellum. "Just finishing up. The colors are eluding me today."

Mrs. Henry put a hand on her forehead and stared into the sinking sun. "It's a gorgeous sight. Maybe too pretty for a canvas. Some things were meant to be experienced, not captured."

"You may be right." Riley started packing up her brushes. "Today, I concede victory to mother nature."

Mrs. Henry waved a hand at the parking lot where Riley had set up her easel. "Where's the rest of your group? I thought I saw at least one of them here with you."

Riley looked around, certain everyone else had left a while ago. "Happy hour." She caught Mrs. Henry's questioning look. Usually the members of the Eastside Sketchers stuck together on their regular outings. They'd spent the last few hours walking through Deep Ellum, sketching the murals that decorated the walls of bars and restaurants that had once been warehouses. Their meet-ups usually lasted a couple of hours, but despite the chill in the air, Riley hadn't been ready to call it a day when the others were done. "They all bugged out to snag seats at the Ginger Man," she said, referring to the popular pub where they often adjourned after one of their meet-ups. "I told them I'd be close behind, but I must've lost track of time."

"Well, go on, girl." Mrs. Henry made a shooing motion. "Remember what I said about living your life instead of just drawing it."

Riley squinted into the sun one last time before conceding she'd lost too much light to get any more done today. She helped Mrs. Henry load a few boxes into her ancient pickup and waved good-bye, happy to have a few minutes of solitude as she packed up her supplies, carefully drying her brushes and rolling them up into a case that she tucked into the drawer of her portable easel. She didn't always bust out paints for these casual meet-ups, but she'd been bristling against convention lately, and her artwork seemed a safe place to express her desire for change. In another hour, this block would be brimming with locals looking for a bite to eat before scoping out their favorite bands, but in this moment, there was a quiet peace against the gritty backdrop of old warehouses turned into a trendy Dallas destination, and she'd wanted to capture this calm before the storm in full color. So much about her life lately had been in the gray zone.

On the way to her car, her phone chimed with the notice of an incoming text and she glanced at the screen. She'd only just started recognizing the number, but she'd refused to assign a name to it in her contacts. Like she'd done every time before, she hit ignore. He could leave another voice message and she'd get to it when she was damn well ready.

The Ginger Man in Uptown was only a few miles' drive, but Riley opted to take backstreets rather than the highway to avoid rush hour traffic. A few road construction signs sent her out of her way, but the longer drive was a welcome distraction. She'd considered skipping their usual after sketch happy hour, but it was Buster's birthday and she'd promised him she'd show. When she finally reached the pub, she noticed she was way later than she'd planned. Another text came in as she was exiting her car, but she ignored it this time. She was glad she'd decided not to go home since it was unlikely her phone would stop pinging anytime soon. A drink and some down time with the rest of the group in a noisy bar was exactly what she needed right now.

The Ginger Man was in a converted two-story house and it was a favorite venue for locals who wanted to enjoy good beer in a casual setting. Buster Creel, the president of the Eastside Sketchers, lived nearby and had insisted they claim it as their designated post sketching spot.

Riley walked into the bar and waved to the few folks from her group she spotted as they called out her name. There was a time when she wouldn't have been able to imagine being part of any kind of group at all, let alone enjoying the camaraderie as much as she did, but these people, although most were amateurs, cared enough about art to not get distracted by delving into each other's personal lives. Buster, like her, was a professional artist, but older and more experienced. He'd been the one to encourage her to join the group when she met him at a showing of his work in a gallery on the south side of town.

"About time you got here. What took you so long?"

Riley turned toward the familiar voice and allowed herself to be pulled into a tight hug, hoping her slight wince wasn't too visible. Jensen was a student at Richards College, and he was prone to displays of affection Riley wasn't used to, but had grudgingly grown to accept because she enjoyed his company. She suspected his affection stemmed from the fact they were the only two out gay members of the group and they both shared a love of lifting weights. She didn't mind an occasional hug and she tolerated him calling her "bro," but she had limits. When she felt she'd spent an acceptable amount of time in Jensen's embrace, she eased her way back to a slight distance. "You know me. I was chasing the sun's last rays."

"No worries. We saved you a seat. And a beer." With a flourish, Jensen produced a pint of dark beer with a frothy head. "Temptress for you."

"Thanks." Riley accepted the glass of local stout and took a deep drink, letting the creamy beer linger in her mouth for a moment before swallowing. She looked around. "Where's everyone else?"

"Darts."

"Ah. And I'm assuming you meeting me at the door with a beer means you already got bounced?"

"Yep. Want to watch the rest?"

"Sure, lead the way."

They walked into the dart room in time to see Natalie, a tall blonde, regaling Buster with a birthday toast. Natalie taught art to kids at one of the more prominent Montessori schools in Plano, just north of Dallas. Natalie always scoffed when anyone asked her what she was working on, insisting her own art was no more than a hobby, but Riley suspected she held on to hopes of attracting professional recognition of her work. Riley couldn't imagine how draining it must be to work with little kids all day and then try to focus on your own work. She taught drawing classes at the downtown branch of Richards College, but at least her students were adults and already familiar with the basics in addition to being able to tie their own shoes.

When the toast was over, Warren, one of the newer members of the group, pointed at the dartboard. "Who's up next?"

The crowd laughed as Buster held up his hands in surrender. "Not me. Apparently, getting a year older is affecting my eyesight."

Warren glanced around, but as he did others held up their hands in surrender. "Seriously, have I beaten everyone?" he asked.

Jensen clapped Riley on the back and called out her name. "Not this one."

"Oh no, I'm good."

"Seriously, Riley," Buster said. "You can't do worse than the rest of us. You may as well let Warren make it unanimous."

Riley tried one more time to shrug off the challenge, but the entire group started chanting her name, softly at first and then increasing in volume at a decibel threatening to take over the bar. "Okay, okay. I'll play." She walked over to where Warren was standing.

He handed her a few darts and grinned. "They tell me you're the one to beat."

She studied his face for a moment, surprised by what looked like admiration. "I don't know about that, but we do come here a lot. Glad you could join us this time."

"Thanks. I'm glad I found you all. My friends have been saying I need a hobby. Who knew I'd get two in one group? And they even rhyme. Art and darts—get it?"

He cracked up at his own joke, and Riley couldn't help but join in with his infectious laughter. She could totally relate. These friends had been a lifesaver for her over the past six months. Without them, she was fairly certain she would've been holed up in her apartment, creating absolutely nothing. But knowing she had friends who counted on her to join them for sketch dates got her out of the house and out of her head long enough to pump out a pretty impressive portfolio, enough to interest one of the more prominent galleries in town, and they were in talks about representing her work. She lined up with the dartboard and took a deep breath before firing her first shot. As the dart left her hand, she closed her eyes. She didn't need to see its path to know it would be a bull's-eye, and in this moment, her world was right.

❖

Claire slapped at her nightstand until the buzzing stopped. She rolled over, pushed up her eye mask, and groaned when she saw the time on her cell phone. Two a.m. Damn. Now that she knew the buzzing hadn't been her alarm, she scrolled to her missed calls and instantly recognized the last number as DPD dispatch. She hit redial rather than waiting for the voice message to come through.

"This is Detective Hanlon. I just got a call."

"Hi, Detective," the dispatcher said. "It's Walt. Got a DB in Deep Ellum for you."

Claire bit back a remark about how as a homicide detective, it would be kind of unusual for him to call her in the middle of the night about anything other than a dead body. "Hey, Walt, thanks for the wake-up call." She reached for the flip book she kept by her phone and scrawled a few notes. "What's the number of the ranking officer on scene?" She swung her legs out of the bed while he rattled off the number and she dialed it before the digits fell out of her head. "Officer Cohen, this is Detective Hanlon. I'm on my way to your scene." While she waited for him to acknowledge her, she shoved the phone against her shoulder and tugged on her pants.

"Thanks. We could use a few more patrol units out here. There's quite a crowd gathering."

"No doubt." Saturday night in Deep Ellum was one of the worst times and places to work a homicide scene. "I'll contact the watch commander. In the meantime, here's what I need you to do." She rattled off a list of instructions designed to keep the crime scene from being contaminated and to make sure no witnesses left the scene, pausing midway through long enough to put on a shirt. When she was satisfied Cohen wouldn't completely fuck up her scene, she hung up, brushed her teeth, grabbed her keys, and headed to the garage attached to her apartment building. Once the phone was switched over to the car's Bluetooth, she called her partner, Nick Redding.

When she heard his sleepy hello, she said, "Wake up, sleepyhead. There's a body waiting for you."

"Go away."

"Not going to happen. I'm headed to your place. Tell Cheryl you'll be home late. We may have a lot of witnesses to talk to."

"Ugh. Okay. I'll meet you outside."

Claire laughed at his grumbly voice, glad she wasn't the only one annoyed about being rousted from sleep. Her apartment wasn't far from Nick's house, and she made it in record time, purposefully driving faster than the limit through the streets of his University Park neighborhood, daring the cops in this rich inner city neighborhood to pull her over. Fortunately, the streets were fairly empty for a Saturday night, which was for the best since as fun as it would be to troll them, she needed to collect Nick and get to Deep Ellum before Officer Cohen had a meltdown.

True to his word, Nick was standing at the end of the sidewalk, shoving his arms into a rumpled suit jacket. She stopped barely long enough for him to jump in the car and then sped off. She pointed at his head. "You might want to do something about that or folks will mistake you for Einstein."

He whipped out a comb and dutifully arranged his bedhead into a passable style. "Tonight was the first night in two weeks Cheryl wasn't called in," he offered as an explanation for his disarray. His wife was a highly sought after OB/GYN, and her salary was the reason they could afford to live in such an affluent part of town.

"Sorry to disturb your night of romance."

"I can hear the sorrow in your voice," he replied, his voice laced with sarcasm. "Let me guess—you were up listening to the scanner and snagged this one just for us. Where're we headed?"

Claire was used to Nick ribbing her about her lack of a personal life. "Very funny. Dead body in Deep Ellum. Don't have many details, but a couple of drunk kids stumbled onto her in a parking lot."

"Homeless?"

She shook her head. "I talked to the officer on scene. He said the body was posed." She handed over her phone. "Cohen sent me a pic. Tell me what you think." She kept her eyes on the road while he studied the photo. He handed it back to her with a low whistle.

"That's weird."

"Yep."

"They already have a crowd forming?"

"They do."

"We're going to need more uniforms on scene."

"Already on it."

He nodded his approval and yawned. "It's going to be a late night."

"Afraid so."

"I'm starving."

She laughed and pointed at her bag. "I refilled this afternoon. Help yourself."

Nick grinned and reached in and grabbed a bag of Cheetos from the stash of snacks.

"Don't get orange all over everything, okay?" she said.

He nodded while he chewed, and Claire smiled at his easy enjoyment of the simple snack. They'd been partners for three years, and in that time she learned that a hungry Nick was of no use to anyone.

"These are so much better than that healthy version Cheryl buys."

"No disparaging your wife. She's my favorite part of you." She turned onto Elm Street and shook her head at the throngs of people milling around in the street. "This looks like a regular Saturday night crowd. I'm hoping they're all too busy thinking about their next drink to notice a crime scene."

Nick grunted. He licked his fingers, and pointed out the window. "There's a parking space by the dumpster behind Henry's

Thrift Shop. It'll be a lot easier to walk from there than to fight our way through the crowd."

"I love how you know all the things. Plus, our scene just happens to be at Henry's." She turned in front of the building and drove down the narrow alley to find the spot exactly where Nick had promised.

"This is where I park when I come down here for barbecue at Pecan Lodge, you know, on nights Cheryl is working late and not policing my dinner with grilled chicken and salad. I know Lila Henry back from when I was working out of Central Patrol."

Claire took the keys out of the ignition and grabbed her notebook from the console. "Let's do this." She stepped out of the car and took a deep breath. She'd seen plenty of dead bodies in her tenure as a homicide detective and even before that when she was on patrol, but she'd made a pledge at the start of her career to never become numb to the very real consequences of the crime she had dedicated her life to eradicating.

They edged through the crowd to the side of the building, and Claire flashed her shield at the harried uniformed cop tasked with keeping order.

"Glad you finally made it," he said. "People are starting to get restless."

"You should have backup any minute," she said. "Where's Cohen?"

He jerked his chin to the right and Claire spotted another officer standing with his arms crossed in front of the colorful mural on the side of Henry's. She and Nick strode in his direction. "Talk to me," she said as she approached.

Cohen stepped aside to reveal a young woman sitting on the ground, her back against the building. Her arms were slack and resting on her crossed legs and her eyes were closed as if she was concentrating. From a distance, she looked like she was engaged in a little outdoor yoga, albeit in a strange spot, but there was nothing namaste about her business suit or the distinct bruising on her neck.

"She doesn't look dead," Nick said.

"You heard him, Cohen," Claire said. "Are you sure she's dead?"

"She's not breathing and she's as stiff as the slice of bread my kid hid under the bed because he doesn't like the multi-grain my wife makes him eat."

"That's super specific." Claire looked at her phone and noted the time. "Anyone call the medical examiner?"

"He was my first call after you," Cohen said. "My partner talked to the couple who found her. They snuck back around the side of the building for a quickie. They noticed her sitting there when they walked by but were too busy with each other to think anything other than crazy lady on the street. When they, uh, finished up and walked back this way, she was in the exact same position and they realized she wasn't some homeless woman taking a rest. They called out to her and when she didn't respond, they got closer and figured out something was up." He pointed to a couple standing about ten feet away. "They're over there if you want to talk to them."

"On it," Nick said. Claire watched him for a second and then turned to take in the rest of the curious crowd. Was the killer among them? Did the victim have injuries not yet visible? Two squad cars drove up to her left and she signaled for Cohen to stand his ground while she walked over to meet them.

She leaned into the passenger window of the closest car to see a familiar face. "Sergeant Lasko, you pull the short straw tonight?"

"Training officer called in sick and I didn't trust the rookie here with his first real crime scene," Lasko said, pointing to the young man in the driver's seat.

"You're in good hands, rookie. Sergeant Lasko was my training officer once upon a time."

"Yep, I knew you when. Why're you still pulling night shifts? I thought you'd be holding down a squad commander's desk by now."

Claire waved him off. "Someday. Someday. In the meantime, we could use some help with crowd control, and we're going to need to canvass to find out if anyone saw anything. The ME isn't here yet, but I'd say the body's probably been here at least a few hours, likely since just after dark."

"Sure thing." He pointed out a spot to the rookie. "And we'll be right there."

Claire walked back to the body, relieved to have another experienced officer on hand. Nick was still talking to the freaked-out couple who'd called 9-1-1, and she took a moment to take in the scene. The mural on the wall behind the woman was a Dallas landmark, diverse faces set against a backdrop of the city skyline. They were a block away from the bars and restaurants, definitely off the beaten path. Whoever had left yoga woman posed hadn't planned on anyone finding her right away. Had she been left for someone specific? Was her positioning meant to send a message?

She glanced up to see Nick walking toward her. "Anything helpful?"

"Not much. They're pretty freaked out. I got their contact info and told them to call us if they remember anything else, but it's pretty much just like Cohen said. Don't think they'll be sneaking off behind buildings to have sex again anytime soon." He pointed over her shoulder. "ME's here. They sent Reyes, thank God."

Claire turned and waved Dr. Reyes over. She was not only the most efficient investigator at the ME's office, but also a friend. "Thank God is right. Hey, Sophia, good to see you."

"You still working all hours, Hanlon? When are you going to get a life?"

"When people stop dying, I guess."

"Anyone ever tell you how nerdy you sound? Maybe you should go out with us doctors some time and loosen up a bit."

"Sure, I'll get right on that. I'm hoping you can tell us something useful before you cart her off. Definitely looks like a strangling to me, but time of death would be helpful. She's in rigor."

"Move over, Hanlon, and quit trying to do my job."

Claire gave her space and watched Sophia put on gloves and start her preliminary examination. They'd known each other since Claire had been assigned to homicide three years ago, and they shared a mutual respect. The Dallas County ME's office had a good reputation overall, and Sophia was not only good at her job, she was a star on the witness stand.

"Any ID?" Sophia asked.

"No purse, no phone. I didn't look in her pockets yet, but unless there's something on her person, we've got a Jane Doe."

Sophia patted the woman's suit jacket, and then slipped a hand in one of the pockets. "I think I've got something here." She pulled out what looked like a business card and a folded piece of paper. Claire reached for the items, but Sophia held them out of reach. "Hang on. You'll get to see in just a sec." She produced a couple of evidence bags from her kit and eased each item into a separate bag before handing them to Claire.

Claire stared at the business card first. Jill Shasta, sales rep for Optima Vending. The card listed an office downtown, less than a mile from where they were standing. Was this Jill or was this someone who knew Jill? Claire pulled out her phone and took a picture of the card. She held up the other, larger bag and stared at the paper Sophia had unfolded and placed in plastic. It took her a minute to register exactly what she was seeing, but she needed someone else to confirm she wasn't going crazy. "Nick, come here."

He looked up from his conversation with Cohen and headed her way. "Find out who she is?"

"Something else." She held up the plastic bag. "Tell me what you see."

Nick squinted and stared, looking from the dead woman to the paper in the bag. Claire watched him digest for a moment. "Holy shit."

"I know."

"What do you make of it?"

"This wasn't some random murder. Whoever did this planned it carefully." She pointed at the bag that contained a rough, but recognizable pencil sketch depicting the exact scene in front of them, sans body. "This drawing was in the victim's suit pocket. We need to find out who the artist is and we'll have our first real clue."

CHAPTER TWO

Riley set the weights down, too distracted by the incessant ringing of her doorbell to concentrate on how many reps she'd done. She'd started the day with excited anticipation about her meeting at the Lofton Gallery later that afternoon, but between burning her breakfast and her interrupted workout, it was turning into a typical Monday. Cursing whoever was too rude to realize she wasn't interested in answering the door, she wiped her face with a towel and glanced out the peephole to see her father standing outside her door. Damn. She should've been prepared for this. After briefly toying with the idea of going back to her weights, she decided not to prolong this confrontation any longer. She threw open the door and, for the first time in fifteen years, she came face-to-face with her father.

Seeing him up close after all this time was stunning, like looking into one of those aging apps she'd seen on social media. His hair was cut close, but instead of being dark brown like hers, his was gray. He was lean with muscle, including his chiseled jaw, but his sunken cheeks signaled he hadn't been eating well, which she imagined was true on a steady diet of prison food. After a few moments of close observation, Riley grew uncomfortable with their mutual stare and glanced away while she struggled to find something to say.

"I know you've been away from civilization for a while, but when someone doesn't answer their door after the first ten rings, normal people give up and go away."

He shrugged. "Giving up isn't my style. I'd think you know that by now."

She ignored the overture. "What do you want?"

"I was hoping we could talk. I feel like there's a lot of murky air between us."

He wasn't wrong about the murkiness, but she didn't want to talk about it. Not now, and maybe not for a long time. "I don't have anything to say."

"Then I'll talk." He shifted from one foot to the other. "Maybe you could invite me in."

He said it like it was a small thing, but it was huge to her. Her apartment was small and simple, but it was her refuge from the real world. She'd holed up here for three days after she'd last seen him, a week ago, and she hadn't even spoken with him then just stood in the back of the courtroom while a judge declared he should be released pending a decision from the DA's office about whether they planned to proceed with a new trial.

For the first time in her adult life, her father was a free man, and she hadn't had adequate time to process how she felt about his new status. She had no idea how much time she would need, but him showing up, uninvited, at her home only set the clock back on her healing. Every cell in her body was urging her to throw him out, tell him not to come around until she decided she was ready, but the teenage girl who'd held her mother's hand while she watched her father being led away in handcuffs still craved the attention she'd lost along the way. Would she ever be able to balance her desire for the father she'd lost with her need to be sure she wouldn't grow up to be like him? Distance was the only way she could keep from being hurt.

But as much as she didn't want to usher him back into her life, she didn't want to air her personal business for the world to see. "Come in but make it quick. I have somewhere to be." She held the door open while he walked through as surprised as he seemed to be that she'd invited him in.

"Should we sit down?" he asked.

"No," she replied, not wanting to give the impression he was truly welcome. "I'm not much of a sitter."

"You get that from me."

"Don't."

"Don't what?"

"Playact the whole father thing." She took a deep breath and braced for whatever it was he had to say. "You said you wanted to tell me something?"

His shoulders sagged a bit and he met her eyes with an imploring gaze. Her mother always told her she had his eyes, but she prayed she'd never look this haunted and lonely. She didn't know this man any more than she'd known him when they'd lived under the same roof. The few years before he'd gone to prison, he'd been absent, a fact her mother had explained away by his demanding job, but during his very public trial, Riley learned his distance had more to do with drug addiction than anything else. Aside from a few vague memories of him helping her learn to ride a bike and teaching her to catch a fly ball, Frank Flynn was a complete stranger, and she didn't know him any better than the people who'd been watching the news of his exoneration.

"A lot's been going on. The DA's office is getting ready to release a statement saying they aren't going to retry my case. My lawyer says if they make good on it, I have a good chance of getting the judge to declare me actually innocent. Then maybe I can get a settlement to help me put my life back together until I can find a job."

She could feel the unasked question hanging in the air—the ask for help, sympathy, something, anything to bind them beyond the bloodline they shared. It wasn't that she didn't feel sorry for him. If the news stories were right, he'd spent years in prison for a crime he didn't commit. The court had overturned his conviction after a series of egregious law enforcement and prosecutorial missteps came to light, but no judge had gone as far as to say he'd been exonerated. The press had been touting the story as a man framed for a murder, but her careful reading of every document she could get her hands on told her it wasn't that simple. Sure, it was hard to believe her own flesh and blood would be capable of a heinous crime, but a knee-jerk reaction seemed out of place as well. If the DA's office had really decided not to move forward with a new trial, his innocence would be determined by a judge's pronouncement followed by the smack of a gavel.

"Congratulations. That's great news." She injected as much sincerity as she could muster, but she could tell by the dejected look in his eyes, it wasn't enough. "What are you going to do now?"

"I'm staying with some friends while I look for an apartment."

She wondered what kind of friends a man who'd just been released from prison would have and decided she didn't want to know. "Okay."

He stared at his worn boots for a moment before meeting her eyes. "I was hoping we could start over."

Her gut twisted. "Start over from when? The day you were arrested? Or should we start from the first day of your trial? Anything before that doesn't seem real in comparison."

"I'm sorry. I know I wasn't always there for you, but I did the best I could. I'm not the same man I was."

"And I'm doing the best I can now." She closed her eyes for a moment, seeking to center. "I need some time to adjust to…all of this."

He raised his hands. "I get it. I know this can't be easy. Believe me, I know."

Again, she wavered. What must it have been like all those years, thinking no one would ever believe you when you said you were innocent? And then suddenly the locks came open and they released you out into the world like the whole thing had never happened, leaving you to navigate a world where not everyone believed that just because the cops dicked around with your case that you still weren't guilty. Hell, she was one of the ones who still reserved judgment. If the police had been correct, he'd brutally beaten a twenty-four-year-old woman named Linda Bradshaw to death, but DNA evidence from the scene that had been shoved away for years, now pointed to a felon who'd been executed a year ago for a host of other crimes as the actual guilty party. The whole thing made Riley's head spin. "I don't know what to say."

"Say we can try. Say you won't give up on me yet," he pleaded. "I talked to your mom and she and I are having lunch next week. Maybe you can join us?"

Lunch seemed like such a simple request. Low-key, low commitment, but the prospect of spending even an hour in the company of her estranged father and the woman whose life he'd wrecked turned her stomach sour. "I don't know."

"Just tell me you'll think about it." He ducked his head and tried to catch her eyes. "Please?"

She wished she'd never opened the door. She was on the verge of getting a real break with her work and now her creative process was about to be disrupted by a swirl of emotions sure to throw her off track. She wanted him and his problems to go away, so she said the one thing that would get him off her back until she could think of a more permanent solution. "I'll do my best."

After he left, she returned to her workout, added more weights, determined to turn her focus inward—away from her father and his needs and back to her own. With each lift, she vowed to get stronger, until nothing could derail her the way his visit had. She didn't have time or patience for daddy issues.

"Are you sure they're open?" Claire asked as Nick pulled into the spot behind Henry's Thrift Shop where they'd parked before. It was now Monday morning and they were no closer to finding the killer than they had been when they'd shown up at the scene on Saturday night.

"Yes," Nick said. "I even called her like you asked and she assured me they'd be open at ten on Monday like they had been for the last twenty years."

"She sounds like a pistol."

"Truth."

They walked through the doors of the aging store, and Claire narrowly avoided tripping over a pile of old typewriters. An elderly woman wearing a smock and glasses perched on the back of her head approached, and Claire stood to the side and watched Nick charm the woman who owned the thrift shop before he made introductions. "Lila Henry, this is my partner and friend, Claire Hanlon."

"Pleased to meet you, Detective."

"Oh please, call me Claire." She forced a big smile and tried to ignore Nick's look of surprise. She never invited people to drop the "detective." "We appreciate you helping us out."

"I'm not sure how much help I can be. I closed up around about six Saturday night and didn't see anything out of the ordinary."

Claire asked her a few questions about where she parked, which door she exited, etc. "Was there anyone else around when you left?"

She shook her head. "Oh wait, one of the artists from that group was still here."

Claire's attention perked up at the word "artists." "Tell me more about that."

"There's this group—they have a name, but I can't remember what it is. They meet up around town and draw parts of the city, and they've been setting up around here the past few weeks. They were all gone last night when I closed up shop except for one. She was finishing up when the sun went down. Nice girl. Helped me load my pickup."

"She?" Nick asked

Claire heard the disbelief in his voice that signaled he didn't think a woman could be responsible for the strangulation, and barely resisted kicking him in the shins. "Do you know her name?"

Lila shook her head. "I know she told it to me once, but you know how you hear someone's name and then forget and then you're too embarrassed to admit you forgot? That's me."

"Can you describe her for me?"

Lila seemed to pull back a bit at the question, her expression now leery. "Surely you don't think she had anything to do with this?"

"Absolutely not," said Nick.

Claire put a hand on his arm to stop him from saying more. "We would like to try and locate this group to warn them about being out here after dark. Any information you could provide us might help with that."

Lila nodded slowly like that was a perfectly good explanation. "She's tall, with short, dark hair. Lean, but strong. She lifted boxes of metal like they were full of feathers. As for the group, I think they have a page on social media, but I'm not entirely sure. This neighborhood's one of their favorite spots, but they meet up on Saturdays, all over the city. They hang out at the Ginger Man sometimes—someone there might know how to get in touch with them."

"Thank you. That's very helpful," Claire said. A few minutes later when she was back in the car with Nick, she started scrolling through the internet on her phone. "Not a lot of info. An email address and details about their next meet-up. Looks like the location changes every week."

"Any pictures?"

"Lots of art, hardly any people," she said. "I'll check to see if they have an Instagram account."

"Want to swing by the bar and see if anyone is around?"

Claire checked the time. "It's a little early still. Let's go by Optima Vending and see if anyone there knows anything about who might have it in for Jill Shasta." She and Nick had met with the dead woman's parents the day before and they had confirmed her identity. They'd also professed not to know anyone who would want to kill their daughter, but they confessed they only spoke about once a month, if that, just to check in.

"Are you thinking the drawing in her pocket was just a coincidence?"

"Not at all, but I don't want some slick defense attorney trying to make it look like we didn't explore every avenue before we settled on a perp. Besides, maybe Jill knew the artist. If she did, one of her co-workers might know about it."

"Smart thinking. Which is why you outrank me." Nick grinned to show no hard feelings and turned the car toward downtown. Optima Vending's main office was located on the east side of downtown in a small building near the Farmer's Market. Nick found a parking spot about a block away. As they walked, they talked about what they knew so far.

"What do you think she was doing in Deep Ellum Saturday night?" Claire asked.

"Date? Although she was dressed like she'd just come from work. I'll admit I've been out of the dating scene for a while, but last time I checked, a business suit on a Saturday night in Deep Ellum wasn't hip."

"True, and why was she in that particular spot?" They'd found her car parked a couple of blocks away. "Chances are good, if she'd gone to happy hour, she'd be there with friends or co-workers. What made her wander away from the action to the side of the block where nothing was going on?"

"That's assuming she wandered off and wasn't dragged down there."

"And no one saw anything?"

"Your guess is as good as mine." He pointed at a door. "This is Optima."

The woman at the front desk barely looked up when they walked in, clearly intent on finishing what was obviously a personal call. Claire took the opportunity to take a mental inventory of the office. An older couch and a scuffed-up coffee table covered with last year's magazines were the only furnishings. According to Jill's parents, Jill had been working outside sales for Optima, which probably meant she wasn't in the office very often except to file reports.

"Can I help you?"

Claire noticed the question was directed at Nick, not her, and Nick was the object of much flirtatious eyelash batting. Best to let him take the lead.

"Yes," he said. "I'm Detective Redding and this is Detective Hanlon. What's your name?"

"Alice," she replied with a slight lilt in her voice. "How can I help you?"

"We're here about Jill Shasta. We were hoping we could talk to some of her co-workers."

"She didn't have any." Perhaps sensing how abrupt she sounded, Alice grimaced. "I mean, we have a few salespeople, but they all work from home. I doubt she's even met most of them. Terrible thing, what happened to her."

"How about you? Did you know her very well?"

"Not really. She came in every other week to pick up her commission check, but she filed all her reports by email. Not super talky either, but she seemed to do okay. Guess she saved all her nice for her accounts."

Claire thought she heard a bit of an edge on that last part. "Would anyone here know if she'd scheduled a meeting with a particular client on Saturday night?"

Alice narrowed her eyes. "You think one of her clients killed her?"

Claire resisted an eye roll. Too much *Dateline*. Of course, Alice didn't know about the drawing they'd found in Jill's pocket, and Claire had no intention of disclosing it. "No, we're just trying to get a timeline of where she was and when to try to narrow down the possibilities."

Alice nodded knowingly. "Makes sense. But no, she was an independent contractor and we don't have any records of her meetings. I wish I could help you," she added wistfully, looking in Nick's direction.

Or you wish you had more reason to talk to Nick. Claire scrunched her brow and Nick got the signal. He handed Alice a card and, in his best imitation of a flirt, told her to call his cell anytime if she thought of anything that might be helpful.

When they were back in the car, Nick moaned about the interaction. "I'll let you explain to Cheryl when I get a booty call in the middle of the night from Ms. Helpful back there."

"Poor Alice. Who knows, maybe she'll think of something helpful."

"Doubt it." Nick looked at his phone. "Reyes sent us a text. She's got the autopsy scheduled for this afternoon. You want to run by the Ginger Man now, and see if we can get any info on this artist group? We could grab something to eat."

"How about later tonight? I've got a lunch thing."

"A lunch thing?"

She stopped at the light and turned to face him. "It's with Bruce."

"And you didn't want to tell me because you're up for another promotion and you thought I might cry at the prospect of losing you as a partner?"

His tone was joking, but the subject matter surprised her. "It's just lunch."

"Secret lunch."

She'd always felt slightly uncomfortable about her friendship with Assistant Chief Bruce Kehler, but he was her mentor and nothing more. "Okay, when you say it out loud, it makes me seem kind of silly. But you will miss me when I get promoted someday, right?"

"Uh, yeah, but I know the deal. You're the department golden child. Why you'd want to move up the ladder and drive a desk is beyond me, and frankly a waste of your skills, but your climb to the top is inevitable. I only hope you'll remember me when you're the new chief. I'm going to need you to make sure my new partner comes with plenty of snacks."

"That's all I am to you, a snack dispenser?" She was teasing and she knew he knew it, but there had always been a little awkwardness around her relationship with Bruce, mostly because

Nick thought he was a Neanderthal. He wasn't wrong. Bruce was definitely old school cop and had very definite opinions about the role of law enforcement and what they should be allowed to do, but he'd steadily risen in the ranks of the Dallas PD, and commanded the respect of the men and women in his command and the higher-ups who'd promoted him. He was like an uncle to her, having served with her father in the Marines, and he'd taken a special interest in her career from the moment she'd entered the academy.

"He's had a rough couple of weeks," she mused out loud.

"The Frank Flynn case? But I thought he wasn't the one who squirreled away the evidence. It was his partner."

She heard the trace of doubt that accompanied the last statement, and she didn't blame him. She found it hard to imagine a circumstance where Nick could break the law and she'd be clueless about it, but Bruce's relationship with his former partner might not have been as close as theirs. "You're right, but the press doesn't parse things out that finely. Everyone who is involved with the case is getting smeared with a broad brush."

"Can you imagine doing fifteen years for a crime you didn't commit?"

Claire knew Nick well enough to know this was his way of shifting the perspective. He was right. If Frank Flynn was indeed innocent of murder, then he'd been dealt a horrible injustice, but they'd likely never know the real truth since it would be impossible to re-create the circumstances of his first trial, now that they knew another man's DNA had been found on the scene.

An hour later at the restaurant, Bruce had the same thoughts. "Just because some other guy's DNA was at the scene, doesn't mean Flynn wasn't involved. He could've been there too but using his college smarts to make sure he didn't leave any evidence behind. It wasn't like we arrested him out of the blue. We had cause." He stopped buttering a roll and shook his knife in the air. "Let this be a lesson to you."

Claire took a sip of her iced tea, while she waited for the crux of the lesson. Frank Flynn's case predated her time in the department, but she'd read every detail she could find on the subject, conveniently avoiding nagging internal questions about whether her exhaustive digging for information was normal curiosity or a search for reassurance that Bruce hadn't done anything wrong. The look on Nick's face when they'd spoken flashed into her head, but she brushed it off. Nick wasn't your typical cop when it came to the thin blue line. He was definitely loyal to his fellow officers, but not blindly so. She liked to think her loyalty wasn't blind either, but she knew she was prone to give added deference to a cop's side of a story, and she didn't see anything wrong with her approach. Trust was an important part of the work they did, and if officers started to doubt each other, their ability to perform their jobs would be at risk, not to mention their safety.

"The courts are getting soft," he said. "Ever since that Michael Morton case, they've been acting like they have to bend over backwards to appease these prisoner advocacy groups, giving convicted felons the benefit of the doubt. We do the best with the information we have at the time. It's really easy for people to come in after the fact and tell us what we should've seen or done. Flynn confessed to knowing the girl and seeing her that night. A jury thought they had enough evidence to convict him." He shook his head. "Maybe they would've made a different decision if they'd known someone else's DNA was at the scene or maybe the prosecutor would've successfully argued that didn't preclude his involvement, but we'll never know now. And with all the press this is getting, any potential new jury pool is already tainted."

Claire nodded. He had a point. A retrial would be shaded by all the attention the case had gotten in the press plus all the attention these types of cases had garnered lately on shows like *Dateline* and *20/20*. She wanted to ask him the kind of hard questions one of those reporters would, but knew it was best not to, so she settled on something innocuous. "How's Danny taking this?" Claire asked, referring to his former partner.

"Not well. There's been talk of letting him go."

"Ouch. Isn't he near retirement?"

"Five months to pension. His wife's not in good health either. This could devastate him."

"I'm sure. What are you going to do?"

"Officially, there's nothing I can do. Unofficially, I'm calling in every favor I have coming and I have a lot."

Claire nodded, silently wondering if he'd ever called in any favors for her. She liked to think she'd made detective all on her own, but she knew she was young for the promotion and a word from Bruce would've put her in front of other candidates. Still, she'd done everything she could to excel and it wasn't her fault if she knew people in high places. "I'm sure he'll be fine with your help. He's lucky to have you on his side."

"But enough about all that," he said. "Let's talk about your future. There's a squad commander spot opening up and I've been talking to Baxter about you. You're interested, right?"

Claire didn't hesitate. "Absolutely."

"Great, I'll set up a meeting."

Claire barely heard anything else he said the rest of the lunch. This was the break she'd been working toward her entire career. A surge of confidence surged through her. She was going to make commander. Solving this case would pave the way.

CHAPTER THREE

Riley had barely cleared the door at the Lofton Gallery when a tall blonde wearing a midnight blue suit that looked like it had been custom-made for her slender curves greeted her. She recognized her from the gallery website as Lacy Lofton, the owner, and immediately felt underdressed in her Docs, jeans, and black leather jacket.

"May I help you?"

Riley stuck out her hand. "Riley Flynn, and you're Ms. Lofton, right?"

"Yes, but please call me Lacy." Lacy clasped her hand. "A pleasure to meet you in person. May I get you something to drink?"

"Thanks, but I'm good." Riley held up her portfolio. "I brought the other work you wanted to see." On her first trip to the gallery, she'd dropped off a sampling of her work which had apparently piqued enough interest to secure this appointment.

Lacy gave her a broad smile. "Excellent. I want to see everything you have, but how about I show you around the gallery first?"

"That would be great."

"The space you're in is designed to whet the appetite." She gestured to the three walls behind them. "We hold the center wall for artists who've been with us for a while because, well, they're a draw. On each side, we showcase our favorite new artists who might not have enough work to carry a full show."

Lacy motioned for Riley to follow her and she led them into the next room. Riley noted with approval the cascade of natural light from windows high on the wall. “This is an amazing space.”

Lacy followed the line of her gaze to the windows. “You can’t see it from here, but there are recessed automatic shades on those, so we can black out the entire room, which gives us a lot of flexibility in the type of installations we can use.” She pointed to the walls. “This side of the room features some of the artists whose work we carry on a regular basis. We rotate their work as it sells and as it complements our featured artists for the month. On the other side of the room, we tease upcoming shows. On the night of the show, the entire room will be dedicated to the featured artist with installations suiting the work. Any initial impressions?”

Riley tore her attention from the art around her. “I’m definitely impressed. But I have to say, most of the work I see here is very different from my style. Do you think your clientele will be interested in what I have to offer?”

“Absolutely. We’ve been wanting to feature a local artist with local imagery for some time, and we think you’re the perfect fit. You’ve captured a different side of the city than what people usually see. It’s like tourist meets gritty local. The fact you’ve never shown any of your work in public before is going to make it even more of a get for collectors. Our clients are going to buy everything you have. Speaking of which, let’s see what you’ve brought today.”

Riley worked hard to contain her excitement as she watched Lacy flip through her portfolio. The Lofton Gallery was the top of her list of desired venues to land her first showing, but she didn’t want to ruin it by acting like an amateur. “Do you have any particular pieces you’d like featured?”

Lacy pointed to a sketch of the old Lakewood Theater. “I’m envisioning a timeline of Dallas, from the older neighborhoods, like this one, to the newer development to the South, featuring a combination of the pencil sketches, the watercolors, and the oil paintings. We could use the installation to highlight the features you focus on in your work, and then show them in the context of the city that surrounds them." She smiled. "I realize that sounds very esoteric, but I have a vision if you'll trust me to execute it."

It was Riley's turn to smile. "You were the curator at the Kimball before you opened your own gallery. Plus you come highly recommended by Buster Creel. I think I can trust you to make me shine."

"You've done your research."

"Always." Riley paused while she debated asking one of the main questions that had been on her mind. "There is one question I haven't been able to answer."

"Ask away."

"Why here? I mean this gallery is amazing, but with your credentials, you could get a gig anywhere you wanted."

"Key word, wanted. I can boil it down to one thing—control. Don't get me wrong, I loved working at all of those places, but at the end of the day, I had a board of directors to report to and a sometimes very, how shall we say, opinionated membership to appease. I quickly learned you can't please everyone, and if you try, the museum displays look like pages from an encyclopedia, and if you don't try, you're constantly being called on the carpet to defend your job. I own this place, so I can do whatever I want." She put her hands on her hips as if in challenge. "Does that answer your question?"

"It does. There's nowhere else I'd like to have my debut."

"Perfect. Let's take a few minutes now and I'll give you more specifics about my initial thoughts. I'll draw up a plan and you can come by later in the week to look it over."

"Sounds good."

For the next hour they went through Riley's sketches and paintings one by one. "Do you have any more sketches of these?" Lacy asked, pointing to a group of paintings of the Deep Ellum and downtown area. "Maybe some earlier renderings? I'd love to display some partially finished work to illustrate your process."

"I'll check. I have stacks of old sketchbooks at home."

"See if you can find some of this particular mural," Lacy pointed to one of the paintings. "It will really resonate with our patrons since it's such an iconic Dallas image. Speaking of which, did you see the news about the body they found there Saturday night?"

Riley pulled her attention from the mural, not entirely sure she'd heard Lacy correctly. "I was there Saturday."

"With the police?"

"Wait, what? Did you say body?"

Lacy nodded vigorously. "Yes. A woman. She was found just below the mural. The paper doesn't have many details." She grabbed a copy of the *Dallas Morning News* sitting on the counter, turned it to the Metro section, and handed it over. "This is from Sunday, but I don't think there've been any new developments. Pretty eerie, isn't it?"

Riley took the paper from her and stared at the photo, which was low on detail about the crime but high on drama with crime scene tape draped in the foreground and the familiar mural looming large behind. She scanned the story, but Lacy was right, either the police didn't know much or they'd chosen not to share anything other than the victim was a woman. Riley shuddered at the memory of standing and staring at that same spot less than forty-eight hours ago. "Definitely."

A couple of hours later, Riley waved to her favorite bartender, Eric, as she made her way to the bar at the Ginger Man. "You on your own this evening?" Eric asked.

"Meeting Buster and Natalie for dinner, but I'm early. Pour me a Temptress while I wait?"

"You got it."

She scrolled through her phone while she watched him pull her a perfect pour. There were a lot of hits on her search for info about the dead body in Deep Ellum, but they all appeared to be reposts of the same story, revealing zero details about how the woman had died or who she was. Riley didn't know why she was obsessed about it, but she couldn't stop thinking about the fact she'd been there, sketching that very same scene, sans body, within hours of it becoming a crime scene.

"Here's your beer," Eric said, setting the glass on a fresh coaster. "Let me know when you'd like a table and we'll get you all set up."

Riley set her phone to the side and took a deep drink, trying to set aside her questions about the woman and ease into the evening, but one detail in the story stood out and she knew exactly why. The dead woman was white and in her early twenties. Just like…Riley shook the thought away. She had great news to report and she wasn't going to let the news mar the telling.

"I should've known you'd start drinking without us," Buster said as he grabbed her from behind and pulled her into a big hug. He signaled to Eric to bring them another round, including one for Riley. She started to tell him she was all set, but then noticed her almost empty glass. She didn't remember downing the beer, but in her distraction, she must have.

After he served their drinks, Eric pointed at a booth that had just opened up. "You all should grab that. Mavericks game on tonight. It's going to get crazy in a bit."

They took his suggestion and snagged the booth after placing an order for way too much food. Once they settled in, Buster and Natalie started peppering Riley with questions.

"How was the meeting?"

"Did they like your work?"

Riley didn't answer at first, enjoying the excited anticipation on both of their faces until she couldn't stand it anymore. "Lacy Lofton met with me personally, and not only is she as nice as Buster claimed, but she loved my work. She's got a ton of great ideas about the installation and my first solo show is set for next month."

"Next month?" Buster asked. "That's fast."

"The show they had scheduled fell through. It's definitely going to be a lot of work to get ready so quickly, but Lacy assures me they can do it and that she has clients ready to buy." Riley took a drink to quiet the voice in her head warning her things were moving too quickly. "Promise me you'll be there."

"Of course we'll be there," Natalie said. "The whole group will be there. I'm so excited for you."

Buster raised his glass. "To Riley. We knew her when."

Riley clinked her glass against each of theirs. "Oh, please, says the man who's had plenty of his own gallery shows. I'll be calling on you for pointers."

"You got it."

Buster was regaling them with stories of his first gallery opening when their food came and they dove into soft, warm pretzels, beer cheese dip, and French dip sandwiches, and for a few minutes it was all quiet at the table. After they surrendered to what was left of the mountain of food, Buster asked, "Did you hear about the body they found in Deep Ellum Saturday night?"

"I did," Riley said. "Paper didn't seem to have many details."

"Horrible," Natalie said. "I can't believe we were in that very spot just hours earlier." She shuddered. "New rule, no one stays behind. I'm looking at you, Riley Flynn."

"I can handle myself," Riley said, play flexing her bicep. "But it is pretty creepy. I worry about Mrs. Henry closing up her store after dark during the winter."

"I know," Buster said. "Last I heard, the police haven't released any new info. Have you heard anything?"

"Nope," Riley said. "Of course, I was hanging out all afternoon with my new patron of the arts, not watching news alerts on my phone. Speaking of which, should we have one more beer to celebrate? On me." She glanced over at the bar where Eric was engaged in conversation with a woman standing in front of him. Riley started to get up and walk over to place the order, but before she could stand, the woman turned and locked eyes with her. She was about twenty feet away, but the distance didn't dim the intensity in her royal blue eyes or the determined set of her sculpted jawline. For the next few seconds, Riley was locked in the obvious interest of the woman's stare, unable to look away and not wanting to. She was powerfully beautiful, and Riley basked in her attention. She memorized every feature, determined to capture the image in a sketch as soon as she was back at home.

"Do you know her?" Natalie asked.

Embarrassed she'd been caught staring, Riley tore her gaze away from the woman. "I don't."

"Maybe you should offer to buy her a drink. She's still looking at you."

Riley wanted to play it cool, but she was unable to resist, and she turned back toward the bar. But before she could reply to Natalie's suggestion, the woman started walking toward their table. Whoever she was and whatever she wanted, Riley was about to find out and she could not wait.

Claire leaned across the bar and motioned to the harried bartender. If she'd remembered the Mavericks game was on tonight, she would've told Nick they should show up tomorrow around lunchtime, but he'd insisted they come straight here from the autopsy. Too bad they couldn't have a beer to drown out the replay of sawed bones and sliced skin from the last couple of hours.

"What's your pleasure?" the bartender asked. "I have a nice coffee stout on tap tonight."

"We're looking for members of the Eastside Sketchers. I heard they meet up here sometimes. Any chance any of them are here tonight?"

"You an artist? I fancied you as a cop."

Claire smiled at his astute perception. "And you'd be right. We're following up on a lead. Help us out?"

He stared at them for a moment as if assessing whether or not they could be trusted before finally deciding they would pass. "They're usually here on Saturdays, but you're in luck tonight." He pointed to a booth to the side of the bar. "Three of them are here right now, having a bite to eat."

Claire turned her head in the direction he pointed and spotted one man and two women in a booth. One of the women stared intently in her direction, and she met the stare without flinching, instantly drawn to her striking beauty. "Thanks," she said to the bartender. She motioned for Nick to follow and started walking in their direction.

"Hi," she said when she reached the booth, her eyes still trained on the trim and muscular androgynous woman who'd been watching her since they'd locked eyes. Her job now was to keep from being distracted by the stirring of attraction. Based on Lila Henry's description, this was the woman who'd stayed after the rest of the group had left the night before, but Lila's description hadn't prepared Claire for the captivating allure of her dark brown eyes.

"I'm sorry to interrupt your meal, but I'm hoping you could help us out." She waited to gauge their reaction, not wanting to pull out her badge in the middle of the rowdy bar and scare off any of the intoxicated patrons. Everyone had a right to burn off some steam, and she didn't want to piss off the owners since she knew plenty of cops hung out here when they were off duty.

"What can we do for you?" the other woman at the table asked.

"They're cops," Brown Eyes said, an edge of distaste in her voice.

Claire nodded and stuck out a hand which Brown Eyes ignored. "We are. I'm Detective Hanlon and this is Detective Redding." No sense being roundabout now. "We're investigating a death that occurred in Deep Ellum Saturday night. We understand your sketch group was down there early in the evening."

The man at the table reached for her outstretched hand. "I'm Buster Creel. This is Natalie and Riley. Yes, we were down there, but none of us saw anything suspicious."

"What time did you leave?" Nick asked.

Buster looked at Natalie and shrugged. "Not too long after five. We came here to celebrate my birthday."

Claire smiled. "Happy late birthday. You have a big crowd?"

"About a dozen."

"And you're sure no one in your group saw anything suspicious while you were in Deep Ellum Saturday?"

"Seems like they would've mentioned it if they had," Buster said. "I can get you a list of names if you want to ask them yourselves."

"That would be great." Claire handed him her business card. She spotted Riley shoot Buster a warning look, but he was busy examining her card. "My email address is there at the bottom. Let me know if you think of anything else. Thanks for your help." She started to walk away, but a few steps in she turned around. "Did everyone leave at the same time to head back to the bar that night?"

She directed the question at Buster but kept a careful watch on the reaction from the other two. Natalie didn't flinch, but Riley clenched her fist on the table, and Claire was certain she'd struck a nerve.

"I'm not sure, to be honest," Buster said, clearing his throat and avoiding her eyes. "I left a little early because I had to run home to let my new puppy out to pee, but I seem to remember everyone was at the bar when I arrived."

He was lying and Claire wondered why. She'd figure it out eventually, but the best thing she could do right now was to let him think he'd gotten away with it. "Thanks very much. I appreciate you talking to us."

She signaled to Nick, and led the way out of the bar, walking slowly, like they had all the time in the world. When they got to the car, she took the driver's seat while Nick started typing on his phone.

"He was lying about that last," Nick said.

"I know."

"Any idea why?"

"Nope, but we'll find out."

"Think he'll send that list?" Nick asked.

"I do. He didn't tell a big lie, just a little one. He seems genuinely interested in cooperating, not the kind of guy who likes to lie, but he'd do it to protect someone. Riley, the one on the left, she's the one who Lila Henry saw after everyone else left. She matches the description perfectly."

"Or he could be lying because he left early and doubled back."

"Could be, but I get a good vibe off of him. Anyhow, his story should be easy enough to sort out once we talk to everyone else in the sketch club."

"So, two possible suspects, but neither one seems likely," Nick said. When Claire didn't immediately respond, he added, "You don't really think Riley is good for this, do you?"

Claire's first thought was that she liked the name Riley, but she shoved the inappropriate distraction away in favor of focusing on the case. She wasn't sure what to think, but when people started lying, they had something to hide, and she had a hunch Buster had been covering for Riley when he said everyone in the sketch club was already at the bar when he arrived. Besides, Riley's body language made it clear she wasn't fond of cops, which usually meant she'd been on the wrong side of an altercation at some point.

Claire mentally ran through the list of everything they knew about the case so far, including the preliminary results of the autopsy. It didn't take long. Jill Shasta had been strangled to death. Her neck was bruised, but there were no specific marks like handprints or rope burns indicating the killer had used some other material to apply pressure. Reyes had found some fibers and was having them tested, but her initial theory was that the killer had used a scarf. Now that they knew how, the remaining question was who, and Claire was focused on the drawing they'd found in Jill Shasta's pocket.

"You saw the way Riley reacted to us," Claire said. "And tell me you didn't notice the muscles in her arms clench while we were talking. She lifts, and unless her legs are super short, she has at least five inches on Jill Shasta. If you say a woman couldn't have strangled another woman, then I'm going to tell Cheryl to take away your feminist card."

"Not even remotely saying that. Just trying to figure out a motive here. Urban artist goes rogue on unsuspecting office equipment salesperson."

"Okay, smart-ass. Obviously, we need to do a little digging to see if there's a connection. We need a last name to get started."

Nick held up his phone. "Checking Facebook now."

"I thought their names weren't on there."

"They aren't listed on the page, but maybe she's tagged somewhere on there."

A moment passed and Claire couldn't stand it any longer. "Find anything?"

"Nothing. I see a group picture, and I think that's her kind of off to the side." He pointed to a figure in the shadows. "But she's not tagged. Most of the pics on this page are of their artwork."

"See anything that looks like the picture we found?"

"Not really, no." Nick set his phone down. "Maybe we should've shown them the drawing. If it's one of theirs, that guy Buster would probably know."

"I thought about it, but I'd prefer to see if we can figure out who the artist is on our own in case the artist and the killer are the same person."

"Good plan. We could double back and follow Riley when she leaves. See if we can pull up a last name with her car registration."

Claire considered the idea and dismissed it. They were early into the investigation and chances were she was focusing too quickly on one person, a dangerous trap to fall into. "Let's give Buster until tomorrow to get us the list of names. If we don't hear from him, we'll get more aggressive. I'm not convinced we're looking in the right direction. It could be a complete coincidence that Jill had a drawing in her pocket. She could've found it on the ground, left behind by one of the sketchers."

Claire didn't believe that was true, but she didn't want to risk missing a clue by homing in on one theory too quickly. Yet even as she tried to focus her attention in a different direction, she couldn't stop thinking about Riley back at the bar. From the moment they'd locked eyes, she'd experienced an instant connection that was at once exciting and unsettling. If they'd met under other circumstances, she might have offered to buy Riley a drink as a prelude to a night with no strings attached—a freedom she hadn't indulged in a while, and one she wasn't likely to enjoy as long as this case remained unsolved.

Chapter Four

Riley pulled another box down from her closet shelf, pried it open, and rummaged through the contents. She'd spent the better part of Tuesday afternoon poring through all of her sketchbooks, but still hadn't found the one that contained the rough sketches for her most recent paintings. This box was her last hope, and she eagerly scanned the contents, a stack of empty watercolor tins, her first portable easel—it was broken, and she'd been meaning to repair it, an empty Blackwing pencil box. She rummaged around, but there wasn't a sketchbook in the mix.

She leaned back against the closet wall and closed her eyes, trying to visualize where and when she'd last seen it. She managed to conjure up a memory of tucking it into her messenger bag the day she'd filled it up when the group met at the Old Red Courthouse last month, but she had no recollection of filing it away when she got home. For all she knew, it had fallen out somewhere and was lost forever. She was disappointed, but not defeated. The sketches weren't essential to the show, but they would've added a nice touch, and she hadn't wanted to disappoint Lacy.

Deciding to give up on the search for now, she put the kettle on for tea and fired up her computer. Her email inbox contained a couple of emails from Lacy with ideas for the installation and she responded to say she'd come by tomorrow to discuss. The landing site for her email contained a running ticker of recent news, and the story about the body found in Deep Ellum was in the feed. The teaser text said the police had released a statement confirming the identity of the victim and that her death was a homicide.

Riley stared at the screen for a moment, wavering between moving on and clicking through to learn more. The water kettle started whistling, saving her from a decision, and she fixed a cup of her favorite blend, letting it steep for a full ten minutes before she added a touch of cream. When she returned to the computer, the story was still there, daring her to read it. Curiosity won and she clicked on the article.

Not many more details than they'd had the day before. The reporter had captured a photo of Detective Hanlon standing at the crime scene that had been picked up by every news outlet reporting on the murder. Riley could see why. Claire Hanlon was incredibly striking, feminine yet tough, and the image of her, in the dimly lit street, against the backdrop of the mural, carried a mysterious air. Riley typed in a few search terms and read what she could find on Claire's background. Claire had recently testified in a case of a man accused of sexually assaulting and killing his victims, and the news outlets described her as a formidable witness, impervious to the sharp questioning of the high-profile defense attorney who'd tried to grill her on the stand. Riley got it, having faced down those piercing blue eyes and knowing appraisal. She sipped her tea and let her mind wander. Was Claire grilling a potential witness right now?

No sense wondering—it was none of her business and not a good use of her time. Detective Hanlon might be beautiful, but she wasn't pleasant. Her hard-charging demeanor at the bar said she was used to swinging her badge around and having folks fall in line. Well, she could find someone else to boss around. People who were supposed to be on the right side of the law had stepped over the line in ways that had permanently altered her life. It might not be fair to lump them all in one group, but she didn't really care. She clicked her way back to the original story and scanned it for details. The medical examiner was still working on the autopsy, but the preliminary report was that the woman had died due to strangulation. Riley instinctively touched her neck and shuddered as she imagined the feeling of helplessness that must've coursed through the woman's body as she lost the ability to breathe. What other trauma had this poor woman been forced to endure before she died?

Riley abruptly closed the website and checked the weather network, figuring that absent some natural disaster, she would find only innocuous events happening there. While she waited for the site to load, she contemplated venturing out to rough sketch some of the locations Lacy wanted to feature, but as the images loaded on the screen, the bright yellow and orange movement on the radar dashed her idea.

She stretched her arms and contemplated her options. Maybe she needed to do something entirely different today. Her mood had been dark since the visit from her father, and she worried it would spill over into her drawings. She didn't feel like being around other people, but a movie might be nice. She switched to the site for the theater down the street and clicked on the day's schedule, but before she could focus on the choices, her doorbell rang. She stared at the door. Except for the visit from her father, only Mormons and telemarketers darkened her door, so she ignored it at first, but the persistence of her unwanted visitor finally won out over her ability to block out the noise. She walked over to the door and peered through the viewer and sighed when she saw the woman on her doorstep. She eased the door open only a crack. "Mom, I'm working."

"If you answered your phone, I wouldn't drop by, but you leave me no choice."

Riley sighed. She recognized the tone for what it was and knew her mother wasn't going to go away until she'd delivered whatever news was so important it had to be told rather than texted. "Come in."

She left the door standing open and walked in front of her mother back to her easel and turned it around. Her mother carried a large, oversized umbrella and carelessly shook it out in her entryway. "It's getting nasty out there." She pointed to the easel. "Why can't I see your work?"

"Because it's not done."

"You let those people you hang out with see your work in progress."

Riley took note of the way her mother put emphasis on *those people* like she was hanging with a bad lot and tried not to be frustrated at the irony. "Those people are fellow artists. We share our work so we can learn from each other."

"I get it. Your poor little mother has nothing to offer and wouldn't understand your work anyway."

Riley wasn't buying in to her poor pitiful routine today. "Please. There's nothing to understand. I'm working on some new pieces for a show. My first solo gallery show." She handed her mother one of the glossy flyers Lacy had sent over.

Her mom awkwardly touched the edge of the paper, and then quickly set it down. "That's so exciting."

She'd said the right words, but they fell flat. "It is actually."

"Where is this gallery?"

"You don't have to go." Riley had a vision of her mother drinking way too much of the complimentary sparkling wine and telling everyone in sight to buy her daughter's little drawings in a slurred voice.

"What if I want to?"

"I'll send you the exact details as soon as it's all confirmed," Riley said to buy time. "But just you."

"Your father would be so proud."

"Don't start."

"He said he came by to see you."

"He did."

"It would kill you to join us for lunch?"

"Kill me? No, but I refuse to do lots of things that aren't going to kill me because I don't want to and there's no compelling reason to do them. Please respect my boundaries."

"He's innocent. He spent years in prison for a crime he didn't commit. Shouldn't that make a difference?"

"Maybe, but it's more complicated than that." This wasn't the first time her mom had tried to nag her into being nice to her father. Angela Flynn might be capable of forgiving and forgetting the many versions of her husband that didn't fit with the current wrongfully convicted model, but Riley's memories of the distant father from her teens who'd cheated on her mother with one of his teaching assistants was vivid and unrelenting. "Please let it go. I'll deal with this in my own time."

"I've forgiven him."

Her voice was low, almost as if she was ashamed to admit how easily she'd slipped back into the time before their lives had been shattered. Riley recognized the huge admission for what it was—a desperate grab at rewriting the past. Her father's trial and incarceration had had a huge impact on her life, but nothing compared to her mother's. Her mother had to find a job in the working world to support Riley and also to pay the mounting debt from her father's legal defense. Back then, it wasn't fashionable to conduct online fundraising campaigns, and even if it had been, no one contributes money to a lost cause.

From what she'd gleaned from her own research, her father had been sleeping with his graduate TA for months, telling her he was on a path to leaving his wife and family so that he could be with her. In truth, he was merely stringing her along to get laid, and medicating his middle-age crisis with drugs and a younger woman. At the trial, they learned that Frank had told his best friend he had considered leaving his wife several times but had never been able to follow through. Riley was pretty sure that was the moment she'd gone from not liking him to actively hating him and wishing he was completely out of their lives.

When the TA's dead body was found, his infidelity was revealed. The police focused on him as the number one suspect, causing him to lose his job, his family. When a jury decided he'd strangled the TA in a fit of rage when she grew tired of being his secret sidepiece and threatened to tell the world about their love, he'd lost the last thing he had—his freedom.

The jury verdict had been swift and the punishment phase of the trial grueling. When the jury settled on forty years of prison, it had seemed like a lifetime to Riley. Her mother had been a real stand by your man kind of spouse, but before the last appeal was exhausted, Riley vowed never to speak to him again. She'd piled everything she owned into the back of an old Ford pickup she'd bought with money she'd earned giving drawing lessons at the local community center and drove east to Denton where she did odd jobs until she started college in the fall. The university was only an hour away from her childhood home, but it was far enough to get away from him, away from the press, away from the stress of never knowing who her father really was—benevolent guy who taught her how to ride a bike or selfish prick who'd fucked over their family.

"You may have forgiven him," she told her mother, "but I'm not there yet and I don't know if I ever will be." She watched her mother tear up and instantly experienced a sting of remorse, but not enough to change her mind. "Let's talk about something else. Have a seat. Do you want a cup of tea?"

"I can't stay." Her mother glanced toward the door.

Riley's stomach dropped. "He came with you, didn't he?" She walked to the window that overlooked the parking lot. "Is he waiting in the car while you're in here trying to smooth the way?"

"What did you expect? You won't talk to him, but I'd thought you'd do this small thing for me."

Riley pushed past the manipulation, but it galled her all the same. "I didn't say I wouldn't ever talk to him, but no, I'm not ready to talk to him right now, and you trying to push me into it isn't going to rush things along."

"I don't understand you, Riley."

"That makes two of us because I don't understand you either." She glanced back at her easel. "Look, I don't want to argue with you. I have to get back to work. I'll think about getting together with him. I'll call you tomorrow. I promise."

Her mother stared hard, like she was trying to divine if Riley was lying to get her to go away. She definitely did want her to go away, but she was also willing to sleep on her mother's request rather than continue to reject her father's overtures if only to keep the peace.

"Okay, but if you don't call, I'm going to stalk you."

"Deal." She watched her mother walk down the stairs and out the door into the rain, but quickly shut the door. She wasn't in the headspace right now to meet Frank's pleading look. Let him be the one to watch and make sure her mother didn't slip on the sidewalk. Lord knows she'd done her share of taking care of her mother in his absence.

Her tea was cold, and she'd neglected to leave the kettle warming, so she started her ritual over again, selecting a brew with less caffeine this time. When she'd fixed the perfect cup, she carried it to the easel and stared at the work in progress, making mental notes to assess her next steps. She'd finished half of her tea and had a solid plan when the doorbell rang again. Cursing silently, she strode to the door, ready to tell her mother or her father or whoever thought it was okay to constantly show up unannounced, that she was fucking working, but when she opened the door, words failed her as she met the intense blue eyes of Detective Claire Hanlon, and her partner, what's his name.

Claire looked up from her desk at Nick who was waving a sheet of paper at her head. "What's up?"

"Buster Creel, the guy who runs that sketch club? He sent the list."

"Really?" Despite what she'd said when they were leaving the bar yesterday, she was a little surprised Buster had complied with their request. "Let me see."

He handed her a copy and stared at his own, running a finger down the list. "There are a couple of dozen names on here, but he underlined a few that rarely show up to their meet-ups, and he put stars by the names of the ones who were in Deep Ellum last Saturday. Should be easy to find your muscled-up friend on the list." He stabbed at the paper. "Here we go, Riley Flynn. This has to be her."

Claire ignored his "friend" remark. Nick had made it clear several times he thought her focus on a woman as the perp was off the mark. He might be right, but she couldn't stop thinking about the mysterious Riley and she was determined her distraction was because Riley might have some connection to the murder and not because she wasn't able to control her own impulses. "Let's run a background check, and then find a time to talk to her when she's not with her friends. We should go ahead and talk to the rest of the people on the list too, and—" A sudden realization stunted her ability to speak.

"And?" Nick rolled his hand to urge her on. "What's up?"

"Hold up. What did you say Riley's last name is?" She grabbed the paper with the list of names off her desk.

"Flynn, why?" Nick asked. A second later, his face scrunched into a frown. "Oh, wait."

"That would be too much of a coincidence, right?"

Nick tapped away on his phone. "It should be, but it's not. She's Frank Flynn's daughter."

"Holy hell." Claire groaned. "This case just turned into a hot mess. Everything we do from here on out has to be discreet. If word gets out we're talking to Frank Flynn's daughter about a murder, we're going to have press crawling all over us, not to mention those Innocence Project watchdog groups."

"Where do you want to start?"

Claire stood and put on her suit jacket. "Let's go pay her a visit. Right now, before there's any chance of a leak." She tossed him the keys and led the way to the car before he could comment on how out of character it was for her to relinquish control of the wheel twice in one week. He'd be wrong anyway. She wanted complete control of any information she could find out about Riley Flynn before they showed up on her doorstep, and the internet was going to give it to her.

A few minutes later, she was wading through page after page of search results from typing in the simple search "Frank Flynn's daughter Riley." Riley had been fourteen when her father was arrested for murder. Fifteen when he went to trial, and she'd turned twenty-nine two months before his release. Claire clicked on Google images and scanned photos of teenage Riley accompanying her mother into and out of the courthouse during her father's trial.

Had Riley been close to her father? Had they kept in touch? How did she feel about his release? She'd never given an interview, never published anything in print or online about her father. Whatever opinions she had about his case weren't in the public realm.

"We're almost here," Nick said. "You find anything interesting?"

Claire looked at him and tried to compute his words. They were driving down a tree lined street in Uptown, and a glance at the dashboard told her twenty minutes had passed, but she felt like it had only been five. "Not a lot. She doesn't appear to have a social media presence, and after Frank went to prison, it's like she disappeared completely from the web. There are some photos of her and her mother from the trial, but other than that, nada. Apparently, she's debuting her work at the Lofton Gallery next month, but I haven't been able to find any examples of her artwork online. The write-up on the gallery's website says her work will be shown in public for the first time on the night of the opening."

"So, the drawing thing is definitely not just a hobby for her?"

"Appears that way. She teaches a few art classes at Richards," Claire said. "But that can't pay a ton, so she must be making some money some other way." She pointed at her phone. "Not much on here about her relationship with her father. She doesn't give interviews and the only quote I could find was 'no comment.'"

Nick pulled over in front of a large brownstone. "How do you want to play this?"

Claire hated ceding control, but Riley's angry reaction to her when they'd first met was a sign they needed to take a different approach. "It's pretty clear I rub her the wrong way. Guess you better pull out your sensitive guy magic and charm her into talking to us. Maybe emphasize she's not a suspect right now, that we're talking to everyone in the sketch club to gather info for the investigation. If we press too hard, she may lawyer up, especially since her dad's been in the system and knows the drill."

Nick gave her a mock salute. "Roger all that. Be nice, don't press, but get her to confess."

Claire ignored his mocking. They both knew she was a hyper control freak, and she'd long since given up trying to change. Her methods meant they closed more cases than any other team on the squad, and her theory was don't mess with success. As for confessions, she didn't expect Riley to break down and admit to killing Jill Shasta, no matter how they handled the situation. Deep down, she was wavering about whether Riley was involved. Riley's reaction to them at the bar could be explained as a natural distrust for law enforcement, a by-product of her father's case. But Claire sensed there was something deeper, and Claire was determined to find out what it was, even if it meant she had to play second to Nick's lead.

The front door to the brownstone was about one-third glass panels, allowing them to see into the foyer. There was a door on either side and a set of stairs that likely led to two more apartments upstairs. Neither of the numbers on the downstairs doors matched the address they'd obtained, which meant she must have an apartment upstairs. Claire filed that fact away with a note to talk to the downstairs neighbors about Riley's comings and goings. She tried the door to the foyer and was surprised to find it unlocked. A newer apartment building would have security in place or at least an intercom, but not here, thankfully. She started up the stairs but paused at the first landing and motioned for Nick to go first. When they reached Riley's door, she took a moment to assess the second level of the building. There wasn't another door opposite hers like there was downstairs, which she took to mean the entire second floor was one apartment, which meant it was larger than most in this part of town. Riley must be doing okay to have this kind of space.

Quit jumping to conclusions. For all you know she has a roommate or... Claire shook away the idea that Riley was part of a couple and actively ignored why she didn't want to go there. She was saved from further examination of her motives when Nick knocked on the door. Claire fixed her face in what she hoped was a friendly, talk to us because we just want to see justice done expression, and waited for Riley to answer the door.

"Mom, seriously—" Riley froze in the doorway and stared them down. "What are you doing here?"

"We'd like to talk to you," Nick said. "Buster mentioned you know the city better than most and you have an eye for detail. We need all the help we can get."

Claire nodded along with him, both proud and surprised at how smoothly he was able to lie. Judging by the slight relaxation of Riley's features, he'd hit exactly the right note. Riley hesitated for a moment, but then she invited them in.

"I don't have a lot of time," she said, standing in the middle of her apartment. "What do you need?"

Claire looked around, in awe of the large open space. A room screen on the far side of the room likely hid a bedroom, and directly in front of it was a weight bench and a small rack of various weights. Floor to ceiling windows let in tons of light, and easels were scattered around the room, all covered except one. She zeroed in on the painting, a few feet from the door. A work in progress judging by the paint palette and jars of water on a high table next to it. She stepped closer. It was a painting of the Eye, a three-story sculpture of an eyeball in the middle of downtown.

She'd seen several renderings of the funky sculpture in galleries around town, but this one stirred a feeling in her none of the others had. Riley had used oil paints to depict the eye, set against a backdrop of a brewing thunderstorm with rolling black clouds and shards of lightning piercing the dark sky. Had Riley been standing outside painting when the storm came up? Had it chased her away or had she stood her ground to document the incredible scene?

Riley stepped closer and stood in front of the easel, blocking her view. "You have questions?"

They were standing close now and Riley's nearness made her agitated. Claire rarely blinked, but disconcerted, she filed away her questions and took a step back. She shot a look at Nick who was watching them with a curious expression.

Nick motioned to the couch and chairs in the middle of the room. "Mind if we have a seat?"

Riley looked hesitant, but not many people could resist Nick's easy charm. "Okay, but I'm serious. I don't have a lot of time. I'm on a deadline."

"Art show?" Nick asked as he settled into the chair, leaving the couch for Claire and Riley. Claire silently cursed him and sat as far from Riley as possible on the opposite end of the couch.

"Yes," Riley answered.

"I think I read something about that. It's your first solo show, right?"

"Yes."

Claire forced a smile. "That's exciting."

"I suppose."

Claire met Nick's eyes and telegraphed her annoyance. It was as if Riley had been schooled in witness stand behavior by a skilled defense attorney. Or the next best thing—her criminal father. Her willingness to let someone else control the conversation was fading fast. "I get why you might not want to talk to us."

Riley turned slightly and fixed her with an icy stare. "Really?"

Claire hadn't expected Riley to warm up right away, but the total freeze was surprising. Claire knew everyone viewed her as kind of a hard-ass, but she thought she did a good job of projecting an engaging persona. She was used to people opening up, not shutting down, when she tried to engage. Back at the bar, when she and Riley had exchanged flirtatious glances, she wouldn't have predicted being completely shut out of the conversation, but she also didn't have Riley's history. What must it have been like having a father who was convicted of murder when you were still in high school? Claire could only imagine the taunts and bullying Riley must've endured during her father's trial, and after his conviction. If she could channel some compassion here, she might be able to get Riley to open up to them.

"Really," she said, not looking away from Riley's intense stare. "Your dad's case is fresh on everyone's minds these days."

Riley kept up her stare for a few more seconds before looking away, but before she did, Claire spotted a slight twitch. Certain she'd tapped into some level of emotion, she pressed on. "Yes, we are eager for you to talk to us or we wouldn't have found out where you live and showed up unannounced, especially after you made it clear the first time we met you weren't interested in talking to us. But I can promise you this—we are only after the truth. Someone brutally killed a young woman yards away from where you and your friends were meeting. If it were me, I'd want that someone caught and locked up as quickly as possible for society at large and for me and my friends who value their ability to feel safe while they roam around the city."

Riley's flinch was almost imperceptible, but the reaction convinced Claire her words had struck a chord. "I'm thinking it's possible you might have seen or heard something you may not even realize is important but talking about every detail might be revelatory. Will you help us?"

For a second, it looked like Riley was about to waver. A slight quiver of her lip, again with the intense gaze. She folded and unfolded her hands, and then used them to push up from the couch. Claire watched her every move, not even looking away for a moment though she could feel Nick watching them from his seat on the chair. Once Riley was completely upright, she motioned to the door.

"It's time for you to go."

Claire was genuinely surprised. She'd been certain she'd tapped into some emotion, that Riley would talk, but apparently the outer shell was harder than she'd thought. She couldn't resist one more try. "Are you sure?"

"Positive." Riley pointed at the door again, leaving her hand in the air. "Now."

Claire caught Nick's eye and gave a slight nod. Together they walked to the door, but Claire turned back before they left and held out a card. When Riley made no move to accept it, she set it on the table next to the door. "Give me a call when you're ready to talk." Then she followed Nick out the door, determined that one way or another she was going to unfreeze the icy stare Riley had cast her way.

Chapter Five

Claire leaned against her kitchen counter and willed her coffee maker to brew faster. She'd barely gotten any rest since being rousted from bed five nights ago with the news of Jill Shasta's death, and for all their efforts, they were no closer to knowing who had committed the crime.

Too bad they hadn't found anything definitive about the artist who'd drawn the sketch they'd found in Jill Shasta's pocket. Claire closed her eyes and pictured the painting of the Eye in Riley's apartment. The stunning image stuck with her, but she couldn't say for sure based on that painting that Riley had created the sketch of the mural in Deep Ellum. Maybe she should've pushed harder with Riley, shown her the drawing so they could judge her reaction in real time. Nick had wanted to, but Claire had insisted on holding back. The sketch was the only real clue they had, and keeping it close gave them control over the investigation. If the press got wind of the sketch, they'd likely make the same connections she and Nick had and quickly learn Frank Flynn's daughter had been at the crime scene hours before the murder occurred. Every move they made would be front-page fodder and any missteps would be magnified and used by a clever defense attorney to destroy their case. Besides, Riley wasn't going anywhere. She had a gallery show coming up, and Nick had made some calls and found out she was showing up to teach her classes with no deviations to her schedule. The best thing they could do was be meticulous in their investigation and the right clue would turn up. She shrugged off a nagging voice in her head chiming in that keeping the information about the sketch quiet also protected Riley from press attention.

Dark liquid started flowing from the coffee maker, and Claire snagged a cup before it finished brewing, adding a dash of cream to cool it down. With the first few sips, the faux feeling of rest swept through her, and she was ready to face the day. She fired off a text to Nick, asking if he'd set up times for them to talk to some of the other members of the sketch group and whether he'd gotten the list of Jill Shasta's customers yet. While she waited for him to respond, she skimmed the local news on her phone. Shasta's unsolved murder was buried deep in the Metro section behind stories about newer crimes, which was fine by her. She'd prefer to do all her work under the radar, even when increased attention earned her accolades within the department. She respected the job of the press and the public's right to know what was going on in their community, but it didn't seem right to be in the spotlight merely for doing her job. Besides, half the time when the press nagged on the department for perceived deficiencies, they just didn't know the whole story and they rarely seemed to care that keeping secrets was part of her job.

Her phone buzzed with a text from Nick. *Two interviews set up this morning. Should have customer list from Optima by the time we're done. Pick you up at nine?*

Perfect. She hit send, downed the rest of her coffee, and hit the shower. While she showered she made a list of things to double-check. Follow up on toxicology report from the ME's office. Review the crime scene photos and check with the crime scene analysts to see if they had found anything new to report. By the time she was clean, she was satisfied they would accomplish a lot this morning, which was good since they were attending Jill's funeral in the afternoon. She didn't hold out a lot of hope it would be helpful, but it would be a good place to observe a lot of people who knew Jill and try to glean some insights into her day-to-day life.

Standing in front of her closet, she selected a plain black suit and a royal blue shirt, deciding that was somber enough for the occasion. When she leaned down to pick a pair of shoes off the rack in her closet, she groaned at her sore back, blaming it on too little sleep and no exercise. Her mind flashed to the home gym at Riley's apartment, and she idly wondered if Riley worked out every day or if she was naturally buff. Thinking about Riley's body caused her own to grow uncomfortably warm, and she switched focus.

No one was in that good of shape without working at it. With the element of surprise, Riley could easily have strangled Jill Shasta and posed her in front of the mural, but why? Motive wasn't an element of murder, but prosecutors liked to build their cases around it, and juries often demanded it to give order to chaos because without motive, anyone could do anything, and it was all so unpredictable.

She shoved all thoughts about Riley, professional and personal, to the back of her head and pledged to focus on the other people on the list, to keep an open mind. She'd barely finished getting ready before Nick texted to say he was driving down her street. She set the security system, locked the door, and walked to the sidewalk just as he pulled up to her house.

"I was going to come in for breakfast," he said as she slid into the passenger seat.

"The cupboards are bare. I haven't been shopping in days."

"Coffee?"

"Drank it all. If you're wrangling for a meal, let's swing through Bubba's and get a biscuit. It's going to be a long day."

"Really?"

"Yes, really. I haven't slept all week and I need a boost of some kind if we're going to keep up this pace."

"I'm all about carb-loading as long as you don't mention it to Cheryl. If she finds out, I'll be eating kale all weekend." He patted his stomach. "She's having my DNA tested to determine what diet would be best for me. I mean, she's doing it for her too, but have you seen her? The woman doesn't need to diet."

Claire laughed. Nick's wife was drop-dead gorgeous, and the combination of her good looks and brilliant medical mind made her one of the most sought after OB/GYNs in Dallas. Nick constantly remarked that Cheryl was too good for him, but Claire knew better. He was handsome for sure, but his best qualities were his sharp brain, strong work ethic, and, at the top of the list, he was one of the most compassionate people she knew, a trait she admired even when his insistence on seeing situations from both sides caused them to butt heads. "Biscuits on me," she said, pulling into the drive-through at Bubba's.

A few minutes later, they stopped in front of a mid-rise office building in Oak Lawn where they were supposed to meet with Gweneth Waters, a member of the sketch club. Claire took one last bite from her biscuit, careful to keep from dropping crumbs on her suit, and handed the rest to Nick who'd already gulped his down.

"Thanks," he said.

"Before you shove that in your mouth, tell me what we know about this woman."

He gazed longingly at the food and sighed. "She's been a member of the group for about a year. Her favorite medium is watercolor, and she likes to spend time at the lake, taking long walks and an occasional bike ride."

"Sounds like a personal ad," Claire observed.

"I don't make this shit up. I found it on her online profile. She's seeking a like soul on several different hookup sites."

"Anything else?"

"She's a bookkeeper for Duncan Estes, the accounting firm."

"Duncan is a pretty big firm. They probably have vending machines," Claire observed.

"As do hundreds of other businesses in Dallas."

"You're hilarious."

"You say that like it's a bad thing," Nick said.

"What did you tell her about why we want to talk to her?"

"I was vague. Said we were looking into some issues with crime reports in her neighborhood. It was her idea for us to talk to her at work."

"Sounds good." While Nick chomped down on his biscuit, Claire ran through a mental checklist of the questions she wanted to ask. Some cops would've been satisfied with whatever info they could find off social media and a quick phone conversation, but Claire preferred in-person interviews for the subtle clues they provided.

A few minutes later, Gweneth, a petite brunette who looked to be in her mid-fifties, ushered them into her office. "I'm so glad you're here," she said. "If there are horrible things going on in my neighborhood, I want it rooted out immediately, and I'll do anything I can to help. You know, a new family moved in down the block about a month ago. I don't want to cast aspersions, but I suspected something was off right away."

Claire exchanged a look with Nick. This could go off the rails fast if they didn't rein it in. "Actually, another matter has come up that we'd like to talk to you about."

Gweneth scooted to the edge of her chair and leaned forward. "I'll do whatever I can to help."

"We understand you were part of the Eastside sketch club that met last weekend in Deep Ellum."

She nodded eagerly. "I can hardly believe we were yards away from where that poor woman was found." She placed a hand over her mouth. "Unbelievable, the amount of crime in our city." Her eyes widened. "You're here looking for clues, aren't you?"

"We're talking to everyone who was in the area that day," Nick said. "It's possible you saw or heard something that might be significant, even if you didn't realize it at the time."

Gweneth rested her chin in her hand and stared at the ceiling like she was thinking deep thoughts. Claire was on the verge of losing patience with her since she was clearly so invested in the drama, it was possible she'd make something up to seem important or insert herself into the case.

"I wish I could help you, but I was very focused on my work that day. Would you like to see my drawings?" She didn't wait for an answer before pulling out her phone and scrolling. She handed the phone to Claire who turned it so both she and Nick could look. There were a total of four photos, each one depicting the mural where Jill Shasta's body had been found. The sketches were better than what she could have drawn, but even to her untrained eye, they were amateurish, and a completely different style than the rough sketch they'd found at the scene.

"These are very good," Claire lied. "How long have you been part of the group?"

"Only about six months. I started drawing late in life, but it's become a passion. I get to combine that with my love of the city, and it's a perfect combination."

"I always think of art as kind of a solitary pursuit," Nick said. "You know, the artist alone in their garret, painting away. How does that group thing work for you all?"

"I'll confess, I don't always like the critiques," Gweneth said. "I feel like some of the others think they're too good for the rest of us, but I'm not sure I'd be comfortable sketching in some parts of town on my own, so there's that. Besides urban sketching is the big scene right now, and I don't want to miss out on any opportunities."

Claire assumed what she hoped was a sympathetic expression. "I can only imagine." Gweneth Waters sounded like an opportunistic busybody, and Claire wondered if the other people in the group had the same thoughts.

Nick pulled out a picture of Jill Shasta and held it out to her. "Do you know this woman?"

"Is that the dead girl? No, I've never seen her before. She was very pretty."

Claire took note of how fast Gweneth answered the did you know her question, but that, by itself, wasn't particularly telling. Lots of people rushed through the topic of death. "We're particularly interested in whether you saw anything or anyone out of the ordinary that day. Anything that stuck with you?"

Gweneth pursed her lips and furrowed her brow in a grand display of thought. "Nothing comes to mind. The woman who runs the thrift shop kept walking around outside, loading her truck. It was very distracting, but I suppose it's part of her job, so I didn't say anything." She lowered her voice to a whisper. "Who knows what was in all those boxes?"

Claire felt Nick shift in his seat beside her and silently willed him not to react. "Did the boxes look heavy?"

"I guess. Some of the others dropped what they were doing and helped out, but I mean we were there to work too, so…" She didn't finish the sentence, perhaps realizing she sounded a little bitchy.

"Buster said everyone went to the Ginger Man after the session that night. Did you join them?" Claire asked.

"I did, but only for a quick drink." Gweneth frowned. "Am I a suspect?"

Claire smiled. "We're merely trying to establish a timeline and it would help to know when the entire group was no longer in the area, giving the killer time to make his move."

"I left right around the time that Buster did. There were about three people still there when I left, Riley, Jensen, and Warren."

"I guess you don't know how long they stayed?"

"You'd have to ask them. I wasn't really paying attention."

Claire doubted that statement was true. "Thanks, we will. Anything else you can think of?"

"No, but I'll definitely let you know if anything comes to mind." She frowned again. "Do you think I'm in danger?"

Nick shook his head. "We don't have any reason to believe this is anything other than a one-time event. Of course, you should be careful wherever you are, but as long as you stay aware of your surroundings, you should be fine."

On their way to the car, Claire chided him. "Do you think it was wise to tell her this is a one-time thing?"

"Do you have any reason to believe that it isn't?"

"No, but it does have a weird feel about it. Like the killer was doing it for sport. That kind of crazy often repeats itself."

"And you'd prefer I say that to her?" Nick asked. "I thought you wouldn't want to stir up the general public without good cause."

"You're right," Claire said. "I'm probably overreacting, but the whole thing with the drawing in the pocket bothers me. This killer was sending a message, and until we figure out what the message is, I don't think we're in the clear." She shook away the ominous thought. "Who's next?"

The next two interviews went about like the first, and Claire became increasingly agitated at the time spent with nothing to show for it. What she wanted to do was track down Riley, confront her with the drawing, and demand answers, but years of ingrained instinct held her back. As they were leaving the last interview, Nick echoed her frustration.

"We're spinning here."

"I know."

"You still want to go to the funeral?" he asked.

Claire heard the strain in his voice. Nick's dad had dropped dead of a heart attack a few months ago, completely unexpected, and Nick had been crushed. She knew he still bore the weight of the loss, and a funeral would only open not yet healed wounds. "Want is a strong word. I think it would be good to make an appearance for the family's sake, but there's no sense both of us going. Why don't you see if Optima has sent their list of clients and start cross-checking it against whatever we have so far? I'll go to the funeral and keep an eye out for any of our sketcher friends in the crowd."

"I owe you. Big time."

Claire saw the gratitude in his eyes and knew she'd never cash in the debt. She didn't like funerals any more than the next person, but she was happy to take on this task to spare Nick any added pain. She checked the time. "Drop me by the church and I'll grab a ride-share home."

"You sure?"

"Positive."

They rode in silence as Nick steered the car downtown. Claire imagined he was remembering his father, and she made a mental note to call her dad and check in. When they arrived at their destination, the steps of the church were teeming with well-dressed mourners making their way into the building. She climbed out of the car to join them. "Text me if you find anything," she said.

"I'm not going to text you in the middle of a funeral."

"I promise I'll turn the sound off and I won't even look at my phone until it's over," she said.

"Liar. You live for work. It's why the brass loves you."

She stuck her tongue out at him and shut the door. He wasn't wrong. Work was everything to her, but unlike him, she didn't see anything wrong with making her career the centerpiece of her existence. Her singular focus meant she would do a better job and rise faster through the ranks than her peers. She'd have plenty of time for the kind of life Nick was talking about, with a wife and kids, after she'd achieved professional success.

Rather than go directly into the church, she found a place to stand out of the way and hung around, casting subtle looks into the crowd. Jill hadn't come from a large family, but apparently, she had a lot of friends and co-workers because a sizable number of people had shown up to mourn her passing. Of course, publicized deaths usually drew a few random funeral goers, voyeurs who actually enjoyed all the trappings of a high-profile funeral, and some of these people probably fell into that category.

She scanned the crowd one last time before entering the church, but instead of nameless strangers, this time she spotted a familiar face. Before she could process her surprise, she heard herself calling out a name. "Riley?"

❖

Riley watched while Lacy leafed through the pages of her portfolio, worried she'd fallen short. "I couldn't find one of my sketchbooks—the one that had most of the earlier sketches of Deep Ellum and the downtown venues—but this lot has a few rough sketches of some of the other spots you wanted to feature."

Lacy looked up from the pages. "These are exactly what I had in mind. If you find the others, let me know and we'll work them in, but we can get started with these for now." She motioned to the back room. "I've got a mockup of what I have in mind if you have time to check it out."

"Absolutely." Riley followed, excited to see Lacy's vision for the show. She'd had a hard time focusing on much of anything since the visit from Claire Hanlon and her partner earlier in the week. She'd talked to Buster and found out he'd shared the list of all the members of the sketch club with the detectives. Hanlon and her partner had even reached out to a couple of the other members of Eastside Sketchers, but she still couldn't help but feel they'd singled her out because she was Frank Flynn's daughter. On top of that, her mother had called again to try to nag her into a "family" meeting. All this drama when all she wanted to do was be completely immersed in her work.

Lacy stopped in front of a wall and pointed at the arrangement hanging in front of them. "I like the effect. What do you think?"

Riley stared, stunned at the surprise of seeing her own work in a new light. The painting she'd sent over yesterday of the Eye was centered on the wall. In real life, the sculpture was striking even in daylight, but Lacy had highlighted the effect with shadows of light and by a large, cascading frame that gave it a 3-D effect. Standing close, it felt like the sculpture was looking into, even through her. "It's creepy, but in a good way."

Lacy laughed. "Exactly what I was going for." She pointed to another section of the wall. "Here, we'll have a display of your sketches in the same way."

Riley noted the use of the same cascading effect with frames in various sizes protruding from the wall to illustrate her work as it progressed from rough sketch to a polished finish. "Wow. When you said you were going to show the progression, I was envisioning more of a one-dimensional exhibit."

"I think this showcases your talent much more nicely. Don't you?"

"I think it's amazing. And I think you make me look really good." Riley pointed at one of the earlier sketches of the Eye. "I'll look really hard for that missing sketchbook because I'm sure there were a few more angles of the sculpture in there."

"Whatever you find, we can work it in. I'm excited about showing your work." Lacy looked away from the wall and met Riley's eyes. "If you want to discuss any other aspects of the installation, perhaps we could meet for coffee or maybe for a glass of wine."

Riley wondered if the sudden shift in mood from professional to personal was her imagination or if Lacy was truly flirting with her. Whatever it was, she was both flattered and anxious at the shift in attention. "Uh, sure, if I think of anything, I'll let you know." She glanced at her phone. "I should get going. I have a class."

Less than a minute later, she was standing on the sidewalk outside of the gallery, wishing she had social skills. Lacy was beautiful, but meeting up with her for a drink wasn't going to lead anywhere. She didn't get involved with people, especially not ones who she hoped to be around for a while. And it wasn't like she could have a one-night stand with the woman who was about to host her art show. Talk about awkward. If Lacy brought up the idea again, she'd play dumb and pretend like she hadn't even noticed the flirting.

In the meantime, she actually did have a class to teach. The drive from the gallery to Richards only took a few minutes, but parking was the real bitch. After circling the streets of downtown numerous times, she finally snagged a spot on the street a few blocks from the college. She used the app on her phone to pay the meter and made her way to work. She enjoyed the continuing ed classes because most of the students were genuinely interested in learning new techniques, probably a result of the fact they were older and they were paying for the classes on their own, unlike the undergraduate students who tacked on art as an elective they'd decided would be an easy pass. Tonight, they were going to explore lighting techniques, a pleasant coincidence to Lacy showing her special lighting effects on her own work.

"Riley?"

Riley looked around at the sound of her name and spotted Claire Hanlon standing a few feet away. What was she doing here? Could she be following her? She started to ask the questions out loud, but people started to crowd around them, and Riley realized she was caught in a throng. She turned to leave, but Claire called out for her to wait, and while every instinct told her to keep walking, she held still until Claire was at her side. "What?" was all she could manage.

"I thought you didn't know her," Claire said.

Riley squinted as if she could make sense of Claire's words if she concentrated really hard. "Who are you talking about?"

Claire pointed and Riley followed the direction of her finger. The church. The gathering of people. She looked back at Claire who was wearing a really nice suit, and all the cylinders clicked into place. This was the murder victim's funeral. "I don't. I'm headed to teach a class. Are you going to the funeral?"

She wasn't sure why she'd asked the question, but she was genuinely curious about the answer. Did Claire really care so much for the victim's family that she'd attend a funeral of a person she didn't know? Was it an act of kindness or was Claire's presence here some clue-gathering technique? Why did she care either way?

"Yes," Claire said simply. "Just the service. I expect the burial will be mostly family."

Riley nodded as if that made perfect sense. "Did she have a big family?"

Claire looked surprised at the question. "Not large."

"Then it's good that you're going, I guess." Riley looked around. "Where's your partner?"

"It's just me." Claire looked toward the door. "I should probably go."

"Me too." Riley started to tell her to have a good evening, but the platitude seemed silly in light of where she was headed. "See you later" seemed inappropriate as well, considering how loathe she'd been to answer any of Claire's questions. "Bye."

She waited until she was about ten feet away before looking back. She told herself it was to see how many people had shown up for the victim's funeral, to pay her own respects for a life lost, but when she met Claire's questioning eyes across the crowd, she knew her curiosity had been singularly focused on the woman heading the investigation, and she knew it had nothing to do with the case.

CHAPTER SIX

The funeral was like most Claire had been to, mostly sad with a few precious, uplifting moments as people came forward with stories of the best parts of Jill Shasta's life, remembered with the hazy glow of hindsight. After the service, the pastor announced everyone was welcome to join them for the burial at a well-known cemetery in uptown Dallas.

Claire decided to pass on the invite. Based on her observation of the crowd and their interaction with the family before the service, she'd hadn't picked up on anyone in particular who merited further interest, and she had no desire to stand outside in the cold for a mini version of the service she'd just witnessed. She hung back for a bit, waiting for most of the crowd to make their way out of the church, and then pulled out her phone to summon a car.

"Detective Hanlon?"

She looked up into the eyes of Jill's father, Gene Shasta. "Hello. I hope you don't mind that I came. It was a beautiful service."

"Thank you. Jill would've hated it." He smiled. "She wasn't big on organized religion."

Claire barely resisted saying "me too." "I've come to learn that these memorials are more for the living. Based on what everyone had to say, your daughter was a wonderful person. I hope that's the memory you can hang on to."

He let out a long breath. "We're doing the best we can." He looked over his shoulder at his wife, who was talking to the pastor. "Any news?"

"Not yet."

"But you have some leads?"

Claire hesitated, hating the part of her job where she had to walk a thin line between being helpful and being suspicious. "We do and I promise I'll update you as soon as I can. I get that it's frustrating, but it's important at this stage of the process that we are very careful about controlling the flow of information. I trust you completely, but you might inadvertently give away a clue that could compromise the investigation."

"I understand, but promise me you'll contact us as soon as you know something." He looked at his wife again. "Closure won't solve everything, but it might help us heal."

"I promise." She shook his hand and watched him walk back to his wife and put a protective arm around her. Their lives would never be the same, and no matter how much they sought closure, nothing she would ever tell them about the resolution of the case would change that.

She waited until she was out of the building before signing into the ride share app. Before she could input her destination, a text popped up from Nick.

Checking the list. Nothing so far. Schedule more interviews for tomorrow?

The idea of several more hours spent talking to would-be artists was mind-numbing. Claire thought back to her desire to confront Riley. She would've been better off skipping the funeral and doing that instead. An idea popped in her head and she texted Nick back. *Go ahead and schedule. Can you text me Riley Flynn's teaching schedule?*

Sure, hold on.

She stared at the phone, impatiently willing his text to appear. When it finally did, she opened the attachment and scanned the document. Riley's class would be over in fifteen minutes. If she hurried she could make it.

Did you get it?

She typed back. *Yes. Thx. I'll pick you up at nine tomorrow.* She shoved her phone in her pocket, hoping he wouldn't ask any follow-up questions, and started walking south toward the college.

The downtown building wasn't large, and she managed to find the right classroom without having to ask for help. She could see Riley at the head of the class through the slim vertical window alongside the door. The students peered around their easels and appeared to be listening intently to whatever it was she had to say. For her part, Riley was animated, her arms and hands waving through the air in a clear demonstration of enthusiasm for the subject matter. Claire was so engaged in watching her, that she was caught off guard when the students started pushing through the door. Claire hung back and watched Riley talk to the few students who stuck around, impressed with her patient follow-up explanation of the techniques she'd been teaching earlier in the class. When all of the students finally cleared out, Riley started packing up her stuff and Claire entered the room.

Riley looked up and met her eyes. "You again," she said with more wonder than annoyance.

"Yes."

"This is not an accidental meeting."

"No, I came here from the funeral. I was hoping we could talk."

Riley looked around, like she was seeking some excuse to beg off or an exit route. When she looked back at Claire, she sighed. "I have a feeling you're going to keep showing up until I talk to you."

Claire smiled. "It's kind of my job."

"Your job sucks."

"Sometimes."

Riley stared at her for a moment. "I'll talk to you on one condition."

Claire hesitated, unwilling to concede anything of substance, but not wanting to blow this opportunity. "I'm listening."

"I'm starving and I'm craving Mexican food. I'm headed to Mia's. If you want to talk to me, you're going to have to talk to me there."

"Okay," Claire said, drawing out the word while she recalculated her plans.

"Don't care for Tex Mex?"

"Actually, it's my favorite. I'll meet you there."

"Great." Riley started walking out of the classroom, but Claire pulled out her phone and started typing the new destination into the app.

"Uh, can you text whoever outside? I have to lock up." Riley jingled her keys.

Claire stopped typing. "Sorry, I'm getting an Uber." She walked out of the classroom and watched while Riley locked the door.

"I always picture cops as hating any kind of transportation where they're not in control."

Claire grinned. "It's true, I'm not fond of being a passenger in a strange car, but it just kind of worked out that way today."

"Well, it's silly for you to pay a stranger for a ride when we're going to the same place." Riley held up her keys. "You can ride with this stranger for free."

Claire was torn between the obviously dumb idea of taking a ride from a person of interest, and the desire to take advantage of a sneak peek into Riley's personal space. Before she could think the decision to death, she blurted out, "Okay. Thanks."

Riley's car was a small SUV. Late model, but not with all the upgraded features like leather seats, sunroof, and four-wheel drive. The radio station was set to the local classical station, and Beethoven's Ninth Symphony played lightly in the background as they drove to the restaurant. Riley navigated the heavily trafficked streets of downtown like a seasoned local, prompting Claire to ask if she'd lived in Dallas her entire life.

"Born and raised."

"Me too. By the way, that's the longest answer I believe you've given me since we met."

"I might be slow to warm up to new people."

"Cop people especially?"

"Maybe."

"Oh, I see we're back to the one-word answer," Claire teased. "Let's just get it out on the table—you don't like cops."

"I have good reasons."

Claire decided not to push. Yet. Riley turned into the restaurant parking lot, bypassing the valet stand in favor of a spot near the road. She waited outside the car for Claire to join her and led the way into the restaurant.

"Hello, Riley," the woman at the hostess stand called out. She looked at Claire and then back at Riley. "Table for two?" she asked with a hint of surprise

Riley cracked a smile. "Yes, two."

Once they were seated and ordered their drinks, Claire waded into small talk. "I'm guessing you come here often."

"You must be a detective."

Claire sighed. "I can tell you don't like cops, but you don't know me personally. I might be a good person. I mean you must think I'm okay because you let me ride in your car and you brought me to your favorite restaurant."

"You have a point. I'll reserve final judgment until after I see what you order."

As if on cue, the waiter approached, and after a friendly hello to Riley, turned to take Claire's order. "Brisket tacos, please. Side of Sunset sauce. Refried beans instead of ranchero." She tossed her menu on the table and shot a how about that look at Riley, who nodded slightly and told the waiter she'd have her usual.

"Oh, come on," Claire said as he walked away. "Can I get a ruling, please?"

"It was close to perfect. Ranchero beans all the way."

Claire raised her glass of iced tea. "We'll have to agree to disagree."

"Fair enough."

"I haven't been here in a while, but my recollection is that the brisket tacos are amazing."

"Truth. And I come here every Thursday after class."

"You have good taste," Claire said. She glanced around searching for some way to get Riley to talk about her work. "I like how they've left the building intact instead of trying to make it look all new and modern. Have you ever sketched the outside?"

"Yes." Riley looked surprised and even a little pleased at the question. "I have a whole sketchbook of my favorite restaurants, and I've painted a few." She pointed to the room closest to the kitchen. "They usually have one of my paintings in the room they use for big parties, but it's being used elsewhere right now."

Probably for the gallery showing, Claire thought, disappointed she wouldn't get a chance to assess whether the painting resembled the sketch from the crime scene. "Nice. Where else could I see your work on display?"

Riley narrowed her eyes. "I find it hard to believe you're really interested."

"Is this another of your preconceived cop notions? Let me guess—we're all meatheads who don't have any appreciation for more esoteric pursuits."

"Maybe. Or maybe I just think you're only here because you hope to get something out of it, and seeing my artwork isn't part of the ultimate plan."

Riley's remark struck hard considering comparing the sketch at the scene to Riley's drawings was exactly one of the reasons Claire was interested in getting closer to her, but she couldn't deny there was something more here. She was actually enjoying Riley's company far more than she'd expected to, and the realization caught her off guard. "Or maybe it's as simple as I love a good brisket taco." She paused and assessed Riley's dubious expression. "If it makes you feel better, why don't you pose the questions? Whatever you want to know." She braced for Riley's first question.

"Why law enforcement?"

"Why not?" Claire heard the slight edge of defensiveness in her own voice and softened it with a smile. "Seriously, I never really considered anything else. My dad was in law enforcement with the Marines before he signed on with the DEA, and his best friend is on the force. I was destined to wear a uniform one way or another, and given the option, I'd prefer to stay in Dallas rather than be assigned to some military base God knows where."

"So you consider the job more of an obligation than a calling?"

"It's complicated. You make it sound like I wouldn't be doing this if I wasn't raised a certain way."

"I guess that's something only you can know."

Claire took a moment to consider her answer. She would not have chosen the word calling to describe how she felt about the job. She was motivated and driven, not simply for advancement, but, as corny as it sounded, for the pursuit of justice. Seeking the truth, routing out wrongs, made her feel good at the end of the day, but it was more than that. It was her duty, her way of giving back to society for the privileged life she'd led. She supposed those feelings made it a calling of some kind. "I like being a cop. I get tremendous satisfaction from helping people."

Riley sucked in her lower lip and appeared to be contemplating a response when their waiter arrived with their food. They both dug in, and Claire was surprised at how ravenous she was, but more so how comfortable she felt in Riley's presence.

After they'd each eaten a few bites, Riley asked, "How was the funeral?"

Claire's radar pinged at what might be prurient interest in the case. "It sucked. I mean it was well-attended, and lots of people had nice things to say about her, but…"

"But it doesn't seem right to have a celebration of someone's life when they're not around to enjoy it." Riley shook her head. "I read she was only twenty-two. That's unbelievably sad."

"It is." Claire scanned Riley's face, struck by the anguish reflected in her eyes. She'd questioned enough suspects over the course of her career to detect the difference between genuine feeling and convenient emotion. Riley's reaction was real, and witnessing it put a wedge of doubt in her theory Riley might be involved in Jill Shasta's murder.

They ate the rest of the meal in silence, but it wasn't uncomfortable or awkward. It was the companionable silence of two people who'd shared the same space many times and didn't need conversation for comfort.

When their meal was over, Claire insisted on paying. "I can't let you pay. Besides, you saved me cab fare."

"Speaking of which, do you need a ride home?"

Claire started to say that would be great but stopped. She'd already acted completely out of character tonight by taking a ride and sharing a meal with a potential murder suspect. Letting Riley drive to her house and see where she lived was crossing a line. "Actually, I'm not going home. I have some work to do. I'll grab a ride back downtown." As she followed Riley outside, the lameness of the excuse echoed in her ears, and when Riley turned back toward her, she prayed Riley wasn't going to press the issue.

"It's not true, you know."

"What?" Claire asked.

"It's not true that I don't like cops," Riley said. "It's only the ones who're more concerned about closing a case than learning the truth I don't like."

"Good thing I'm not one of those."

"I hope not."

Riley didn't wait for a response before walking to her car, leaving Claire to stare at her back, wondering if Riley thought she was one of the good ones. She waited until Riley was in her car and out of the parking lot before she pulled out her phone to get a ride. The Uber driver chatted incessantly the entire ride to the station, but Claire barely heard a word he said, unable to focus on anything other than her desire to know more about Riley Flynn. Much more.

CHAPTER SEVEN

Riley paced in front of the diner wishing she hadn't agreed to this meeting. Letting a police detective invade her regular dinner spot had already added disruption to her usual routine. Meeting her parents for lunch the next day was piling on. Of course, dinner with Claire had been more of a pleasure than a burden. She'd enjoyed their gentle sparring, and after the push and pull was out of the way, they'd actually had a pleasant evening. The only drawback was how much sharing a meal with a smart, attractive woman reminded her of how lonely her life had become. Aside from her outings with the sketch club, she had no social life. Dating was a nonstarter. By date three, without exception, every woman started asking personal questions about family and background. Some even guessed she was Frank Flynn's daughter, and Riley's steadfast refusal to talk about her father stalled any forward momentum. With Claire, she didn't have to delve into the past because Claire knew it all or thought she did anyway.

Riley checked the time. They were fifteen minutes late, and she deemed that a good enough excuse to bail. She was several yards away from the restaurant, when she heard her mother call her name. Damn.

She took her time walking back toward them, stymied at the sight of them walking arm in arm. They looked like a happy couple headed to share a meal. She had to dig really deep to come up with a memory of when her parents had looked this cozy. In the year or two before Frank was arrested, their interactions had consisted of whispered arguments behind closed doors about why he'd spent nights away from home without telling her coupled with accusations that he was putting their money up his nose. When Riley asked questions, her mother made excuses for her father's absence, determined not to mar Riley's image of her father, but the day he was arrested for Linda Bradshaw's murder everything changed.

"I'm sorry we're late," her mother said. "It was my fault. I've been meaning to have the engine light in the car checked out, and it wouldn't start this morning. I had to call your father to pick me up."

Riley figured it was likely Frank who'd made her late, but she didn't bother arguing the point. Her mother's codependence was legend, and she'd long since given up getting her to see Frank for the mess he was. She strongly doubted prison had changed him for the better. "We should go on in. I don't have a lot of time."

A waitress led them to a booth in the back of the diner. Riley had purposefully picked this place down the road from the criminal courthouse because it wasn't in her usual rotation. She'd only been here once before and the food was good, but she was unlikely to run into anyone she knew. The three of them settled into the booth and gave their drink orders to the waitress. She'd barely left them to peruse the menu, when Riley set hers aside and folded her hands on the table.

"You already know what you want?" her mother asked. "Frank, I read online that the smothered chopped steak is delicious. I think I'll have that with mashed potatoes and fried okra. Riley, do you think that sounds good?"

She knew her mother rambled when she was nervous, but she wasn't in the mood to calm anyone's nerves other than her own today. All she wanted to do was get this little family charade over with as quickly as possible. She faced her father square on. "I agreed to meet you and hear what you have to say. Let's get this over with."

"Riley," her mother hissed. "Be nice."

Riley kept her voice low, but firm. "No, Mom. I don't have to be nice. I'm a grown woman with a life of my own. I've spent years working hard to live outside the shadow of being Frank Flynn's daughter, but I can never seem to escape." She directed her next remarks to him. "If you didn't kill that woman, I'm glad you're no longer in prison, but that doesn't change the fact you weren't there when I needed you to be. I can't help but wonder if you would've been arrested for murder if you hadn't been cheating on your wife and spending any extra money we had to buy drugs. All I do know is that I've spent the better part of my life without a father, and I don't need one now."

She could feel her voice start to choke, and she stopped talking to keep from compounding her own discomfort. Frank had dropped his gaze to the table while she was talking, but when she finished, he met her eyes.

"You're right. You don't need a father. You've made a good life for yourself. You teach, you're an artist. I remember when you used to draw me pictures to tell me about your day. I still have one, and it got me through some really rough times." He shifted in his seat. "I don't deserve your trust, but I'd like a chance to earn it back. I realize you may not even believe that I'm innocent."

He pulled out a card and slid it across the table. "This is my attorney. Her firm handled my appeal pro bono. She can tell you anything you want to know about the case. I cheated on your mother, and that was a terrible thing to do. I also abused drugs, which compounded my bad decision-making. I can't make up for my past. I can only change my future. I've been clean and sober for fifteen years, but I've never been a murderer. I'm going to spend the rest of my life doing two things—working to make sure this doesn't happen to anyone else and earning back your trust."

He sounded earnest and sincere, and Riley wanted to believe him. The little girl within remembered when he would come home from work and scoop her up in his arms and listen to the tales of her day before he did anything else. She would show him her drawings, and he would ooh and ahh over them like they were fine works of art. She'd loved that man with every fiber of her being. Was there a shred of him still in existence or was the man seated across from her now only a shadow of his former self, with all the substance lost to unfortunate circumstance and the unkind passage of time?

She wanted to believe his contrition was real, but she wasn't there yet. "I don't think I'm ready to forgive you."

He nodded, his eyes reflecting her sadness. "Understood. How about today we simply share a meal, and then, if it goes okay, we can try this again another day. Keep it small until you're ready to take a bigger step."

His proposal sounded good and easy and fair, but also hard and scary and uncertain. She knew her unwillingness to either let the past go or find some amicable resolution held her back in so many ways, but her current condition was a known, and right now the familiar was comforting and secure. Besides, she suspected that the very fact she was his daughter was likely the reason Claire was snooping around in her life. Reestablishing a relationship with him now seemed fraught with more danger.

Still, he was her father, and, by all accounts, he wasn't a murderer. Just like she wanted to be afforded the benefit of the doubt, she owed him some leeway, but she didn't owe him much. "Let's eat lunch, but that's all I'm ready for right now. If you want more, you're going to have to be patient and not push me."

"Oh, Riley," her mother said, her voice quivering with excitement. "That's—"

Frank interrupted. "That's all I can ask. I promise I won't push." He shot a pointed look at her mother. "*We* won't push."

The rest of the meal was spent exchanging surface level conversation. Frank mentioned he'd seen the news about her gallery show and he asked insightful questions about her work and the installation. At times during the back and forth, Riley slipped into a comfortable lull, imagining what their life could've been, but then something would come up that related to the years missed and why, and her guard would go back up. She might be willing to forgive, but she wasn't sure she would ever forget.

❖

The call came in at eleven forty-five a.m. as they were driving along rain-soaked streets toward East Dallas to interview another one of the members of the sketch club. Nick answered the phone, and after a few "uh-huhs" and a "be right there" he disconnected the call. "Change of plans."

"What's up?" Claire asked, slowing the car for the red light ahead.

"We have another body. It's at Large Marge."

"You've got to be kidding me." Claire knew he wasn't, but she held out hope the report was a mistake. Large Marge was the local nickname for the Margaret Hunt Hill cable-stayed bridge over the Trinity River adjacent to downtown. She prayed the body on the bridge had nothing to do with the case they were working because if they were related, then their problems were about to increase exponentially. At the intersection, she whipped the car around and headed back toward downtown. "Who's on the scene? Do we trust them? This rain's going to wash away evidence, they need to—"

Nick held up a hand and pointed to the phone at his ear. "Ron Blake," he whispered and then returned to his conversation with dispatch. The next few minutes of the drive consisted of Claire racing through the holes in traffic while Nick contacted the officers on scene and gave them detailed instructions about locking the entire area down. When they reached the east entrance to the bridge, Claire hunted down a place to park and leapt from the car. She flashed her shield at the uniformed officer standing next to a handful of orange cones formed into a makeshift barricade. "Where's Blake?"

The officer blinked at her for a moment like he was trying to decide if he should divulge the location of his superior. "He's expecting me," Claire said. "Detective Hanlon."

"Yes, of course." He pointed in the direction of the bridge where another patrol cop was directing traffic to turn around and head west before exiting the bridge. "Body's over that way."

Claire spotted Blake kneeling about twenty feet away. He waved and called out to her, but she couldn't hear him over the sound of the honking horns from the traffic jammed up on the bridge. "You're going to need help with this traffic flow. Call dispatch and tell them you need backup. They should be able to get a few more units out here to help direct traffic."

With that piece of advice, she left him to his work and headed over to where Sergeant Blake was standing about twenty feet away. She was halfway there when she heard Nick call out to her. "Wait up."

She slowed but didn't stop, and a few seconds later, he was by her side. "Reyes is on the way," he said.

"Good." She sped up until they reached Blake who stood to greet her. He was wearing a Dallas PD rain cape and rain boots.

"Hey, Hanlon," he said. "Hope you're ready to get muddy."

She looked directly behind him but didn't see a body. "Tell us what you've got."

"Twenty-something, white female. Near the pedestrian entrance to the bridge. We set up a tarp but were careful not to tramp all over the scene."

"Who found her?"

He pointed at a tall, thin white man dressed in expensive, name-brand running attire standing a few feet away, talking to another officer. "Will Gentry. He's a tax lawyer. Crazy fuck likes to take a run at lunch and has a penchant for this damn monstrosity of a bridge. Parked on the west side and ran across. Says he spotted the vic as he turned to head back. He looks on the up-and-up, but it's a weird day to be out running, if you ask me."

Judging by his round belly, Claire figured any day was a bad day for Blake to be out running, but he had a point. "I want to see the victim first, but don't let him go yet." She looked up. "Aren't there cameras on this bridge?"

Nick answered. "Traffic cams for sure. Not certain if they'd pick up that area, but I'll make the call to get the footage saved. Whoever did this might have driven away from the scene, and we should be able to get the tags on all the cars that have come through here."

"Make a note once we have the time of death to request all footage for several hours on either side." She lowered her voice. "And keep an eye on the crowd. Whoever it was may still be here." She took a look around as she spoke, scanning the cars and people who'd gathered and feeling a tinge of relief not to see any signs of Riley Flynn in the crowd.

"Let's take a look. Blake, please stay here and send Reyes when she gets here." She walked off before he could offer any commentary on what she was about to see. She'd rather experience the scene firsthand with no preconceived notions.

The woman was posed, her back against a dirt mound. Her legs were crossed and her hands were resting on her knees. From a distance it looked like she was meditating or in the middle of a yoga class. The only indication something was wrong was the fact she didn't move at all as they approached. Claire bent down to get a closer look when a voice startled her out of her observations.

"You kids planning to start without me?"

"Are you trying to give me a heart attack?" Claire breathed deep. "Seriously, Reyes. I'm glad you're here, but give a girl a warning why don't you."

"Sorry not sorry. I was having lunch a block from here." She pointed at the body. "This looks a little too familiar."

"I know." Claire stepped to the side. "Can you check her pockets first?"

"Sure, Detective. Whatever you want."

Reyes stepped forward and donned a pair of gloves. She started to reach into the left jacket pocket of the victim but stopped and cocked her head.

"What's wrong?" Nick asked.

"Hang on." Reyes started touching the body in several places, making clucking sounds and narrowing her eyebrows. "Blake tell you anything about when he arrived on the scene?"

"No, but I didn't ask much. You know me," Claire said.

"Like to see it for yourself. I know, I know." Reyes motioned for her to come closer. "Check this out." She took Claire's gloved hand and placed it on the dead woman's arm which was incredibly stiff.

"She's in rigor."

"Full on." Reyes pointed to the ground around them. "No sign of a struggle. My guess is she was brought here exactly like this."

Claire's brain started firing with her amateur, but experienced knowledge of rigor mortis and time of death. Based on the stiffness of this body, death had occurred hours before, maybe even as early as last evening. It had been a cold night and had rained off and on. Had this body been here the whole time or had someone dropped it here today?

"How about those pockets?" she asked.

Reyes reached into the jacket pocket. "Nothing here. Let me check the other one." She reached over and carefully unzipped the other pocket and slipped her hand in. "Got something."

Claire dropped to a squat and held her umbrella over the body while Reyes pulled a folded piece of paper from the dead woman's pocket. Reyes handed it to her. "No, you open it," Claire said. She held her breath while Reyes unfolded the paper and held it up for Claire and Nick to see. Claire stared for a moment and then squeezed her eyes shut, hoping when she opened them again, the image would change.

It didn't. Reyes was holding a rough, yet detailed sketch of the bridge from the vantage point they were standing in right now. Whoever killed Jill Shasta killed this woman too, and they were leaving clues. Big, mysterious, aggravating clues.

Claire's stomach soured as a thought occurred to her, but she had to be sure before she could pinpoint the source of her dread. "We're going to need to know time of death ASAP."

"I can get the autopsy done tonight, but I can tell you right now it's been hours."

"Any idea how many?" Claire knew she was asking a lot since they were standing outside in the rain and Reyes had barely had a chance to examine the body, but she had to know as much as she could as soon as she could.

"Don't quote me on this, but it could be as early as last night. I'll know more once the effects of rigor start to dissipate."

Damn. A train of thoughts careened around the bend, tilting on dangerous curves in the form of unanswered questions like where Riley had gone last night after they'd parted ways. Claire found herself hoping Riley had an alibi and even as she did, she realized if Riley was questioned about her whereabouts last night, the dinner they'd shared would be a big chunk of the story.

CHAPTER EIGHT

"You're saying Frank Flynn's daughter is a suspect in the murder of two young women?" Bruce Kehler asked in a bellowing voice.

Claire paused a beat before answering. She'd dropped Nick at the station after they'd left the scene, telling him she needed to run a personal errand, which consisted of a trip to Riley's apartment, hoping to talk to her about where she'd gone last night after they parted ways. Before she could return, Bruce had shown up at the office, demanding answers about the state of the investigation in light of the new body. He'd cornered Nick and bullied him into revealing that their only real clue was a sketch and they were talking to the members of the sketch club to determine if any of them might have been involved.

When Bruce recognized Riley's name on the list, he focused on her as the most likely suspect. Nick had texted Claire to get back to the office as soon as possible, and by the time she walked back in, Bruce was worked up into a frenzy over the prospect of putting another Flynn behind bars. When he insisted on talking to her alone, she wished she'd stayed away.

She chose her words carefully, trying desperately to ignore the rising tide of panic she felt. "I'm saying that Riley Flynn has been a person of interest in the case. As have several other people. We've been holding back on producing the sketches to the press.

So far, we've managed to keep a lid on the similarities in the two murders, and I'd like to keep it that way as long as possible. It's possible the sketches were Riley's. However, the MO of both of these killings fits a man more than a woman."

"Really? Claire, that doesn't sound like you. What happened to all the equal opportunity stuff you're always spouting?"

She bristled at his tone but kept her cool. "I'm as equal opportunity as anyone, but the physical evidence makes it pretty clear this body was carried to the scene." She relayed the information Reyes had provided at the scene. "Yes, another woman could've strangled her, but lifting and carrying her body from place to place is a whole other thing."

"Not if she had help. Maybe she's in business with her father."

Claire wanted to dismiss the idea out of hand. Frank Flynn had been released from prison, but his case was officially still pending until the DA's office made a formal announcement. He would have to be the stupidest man alive to commit two new murders while waiting to hear about his total exoneration, but she wouldn't be doing her job if she didn't at least explore the possibility.

Like everyone else who watched the news, she knew certain details of Frank Flynn's case—more than most because of Bruce's involvement, but she hadn't memorized the specifics. The one detail that stood out was that his alleged victim was a twenty-something white woman. Coincidence? Maybe, but she needed to know more if she was going to seriously consider the possibility he might be involved in these killings. She already knew Bruce's version would understandably come with a certain slant, so she decided to talk to the conviction integrity prosecutor at the DA's office to get a picture of the overall case. "I promise you, we're exploring every possibility, but if we publicly announce we're focused on Frank Flynn or his daughter, then the press is going to go nuts and they'll both lawyer up. We'll lose any opportunity we have to quietly build our case. The press is already going to get worked up over two young white women being murdered. Let's not add to the feeding frenzy just yet."

"What about the drawings?" Bruce asked.

"What about them?"

"Any leads on where they might strike next based on those?"

"We're working on it." She and Nick had been talking about exactly that when they'd left the scene. First, she needed to confirm whether the sketch club had ever had one of their meet-ups at the bridge. If they had, then it was possible she and Nick could make some predictions based on other places the club had gathered. But all of these suppositions were based on the assumption one of the sketch club members was the artist. It might be time to go public with the sketch to try to flush the killer out of hiding, but she'd make that decision with Nick and not because they were under pressure from Bruce. "If we learn anything new, I promise you'll be the first call I make."

"I hope so. I have to be in court next week on Flynn's case and if he's involved in this, that's ammo we can use to sway the judge not to let the guy skate." He stepped closer and clapped a hand on her shoulder. "I've been talking up your promotion. A quick arrest on this case could pave the way. You understand?"

"I do."

"Good," he said, already headed to the door. "Keep me posted."

He was no sooner out the door when Nick reappeared. "Where did you slink off to?" Claire asked. "And why the hell did you tell him anything about this case?"

"Uh, since he's high enough up the food chain to be the boss of both of us. Besides, it wasn't like you were here to run interference." Nick narrowed his eyes. "You and your mentor on the outs? And speaking of slinking off, where were you when he showed up?"

Despite their closeness, she'd never shared every detail of her life with Nick, but she'd never lied to him either. But telling him she'd been out looking for Riley and why would mean she'd have to tell him about seeing Riley last night. He'd wonder why she hadn't told him in the first place if the meeting was pure business, and she didn't have a good response. The situation was complex, and while she usually rose to a challenge, she only wanted to avoid the thicket her omissions had created. She'd find a way to tell him later, but in the meantime, they needed to arrest the killer before they struck again.

"Any word on the cameras at the bridge?"

"Yes, but it's not good. They capture the area near where the body was found, but they don't fan out wide enough to view the scene. I've got the computer guys running all the plates of the cars that night through the system to see if we get a match on anyone in the sketch club or any that worked with these women or are in their immediate circle. Other than that, searching plates is worse than trying to find a needle in a haystack." He took out his phone and pulled up a photo of the scene. "Whoever it was could've parked their car right here and completely avoided being captured on camera. Forensics found tire tracks and they should have some info to us soon."

"Like the killer knew there was a camera there."

"Exactly."

"Any luck on finding her phone?"

"No. We've been pinging it, but it could be anywhere by now."

Damn. Claire had held out hope that if they'd been able to locate the victim's phone, they might be able to use her location info to determine where she'd been last before she wound up at the bridge. "Keep trying. You never know."

"What's going on?"

She heard the concerned tone in his voice, but it only aggravated her. "Nothing."

"What did Bruce say to you?"

"What's your beef with him?"

Nick raised his hands in surrender. "No beef here. Just a guy checking in with his partner to make sure they're both on the same page about the case they're working."

She could see the concern in his eyes and knew she needed to rein in her anxiety. Take a deep breath, think this through. There was only one right way to handle an investigation. Step by step, careful and meticulous—that was her hallmark and the reason the DA's office loved putting her on the stand. They never had to worry about surprises during cross-examination: missed clues, sloppy record keeping, and never ever would she participate in a cover-up designed to lead investigators in a different direction. She needed to tell Nick about her interactions with Riley, and she would, but first she wanted to talk to Riley and get her own assessment of whether she was capable of these heinous murders. In the meantime, she had another assessment to make.

"Tell me everything you know about Frank Flynn and his case," she said.

Nick looked surprised at the change in subject. "Really? I thought you were the resident expert."

"In a vacuum. I'm interested in your perspective."

"Okay," he said. "But not here. P.S. I'm starving. Okay if we grab a late lunch?"

Claire got it. Talking about whether other cops had fucked up a case was best done somewhere other than while standing in the middle of a room full of them. She grinned to add some levity. "I should've known there would be food involved. Bring the list of the rest of the sketch club members we haven't talked to yet, and we'll go through that too."

On the way to the car, Claire was already starting to calculate how she could sneak off later and find Riley to confront her about where she'd gone after they parted ways the night before. She felt another twinge of guilt for not sharing more info with Nick, but her desire to confront Riley was mixed up with feelings that were decidedly unprofessional, and until she sorted that out, she wasn't sharing anything with anyone.

Nick picked his favorite barbecue place, Pecan Lodge, which, thankfully, wasn't near the courthouse and therefore wasn't packed with cops and courthouse personnel. Because it was after the lunch rush, they scored a decent spot in the long line that had become a tradition at this spot, and after a tolerable wait, they made it to the counter to order their food. Once they were seated, Claire looked around to make sure there was no one there they knew. "Okay, give it to me. I know you're up on this case."

"Just a sec." Nick shoveled a forkful of brisket into his mouth and moaned. "This is heaven."

Claire stared at her own plate. She knew the barbecue here was perfection, but she had a hard time summoning an appetite after spending time with a dead body, not to mention everything else that was on her mind. She needed to see Riley and she needed to make progress on this case. She rolled her hand to urge him along. "Frank Flynn's case. You know it inside and out?"

"I do, but probably no more than you, and not out of any desire to try to bring down your good buddy. I took that conviction integrity seminar last year, and these kinds of cases have always fascinated me. Specifically, how do innocent people get convicted and what can I do to make sure I never wind up being the cop on the stand trying to explain why I was certain I'd arrested the right person when the evidence clearly points the other way."

"Same." She had similar thoughts, but rarely voiced them out loud as if doing so would manifest the problem. At some point in every case, she had to decide to go all in on the decisions she'd made or she wouldn't make a very convincing witness on the stand. Wavering convictions on the part of the lead detective led to a low conviction rate, and prosecutors might hesitate to go to trial on cases with detectives they couldn't count on for fear an uncommitted witness would tank the case. She wanted to see justice done as much as the next person, but the truth was that unless there was a reliable eyewitness at the scene when the bad act went down, then the only two people who definitively knew what happened were the defendant and the victim, and on the cases she worked, the victims were no longer capable of telling their side of the story. "But this appeared to be an open-and-shut case."

"Sure," he said. "If you only looked at Flynn." Nick started ticking facts off on his fingers. "He was a professor and the victim was his TA. He admitted they'd once had a relationship. He'd been seen with the victim off campus earlier the same evening. He tested positive for drugs. He admitted he was angry with her because she'd threatened to tell his wife about the affair."

"We've arrested people on less than that," Claire pointed out.

"Sure, we have, but I feel pretty confident that we've never done it without exploring many other possibilities first. There were a number of things the detectives on Flynn's case ignored." Again, with the fingers. "The method, strangling, and the profile of the victim, age, build, etc., were similar to the specifics of another death several weeks before that happened when Frank Flynn was out of town and had a rock-solid alibi. Both murders fit the profile of Milo Shaw, who'd recently been released from prison. He was on parole for wait, you guessed it—the murder of a twenty-something, white woman, who surprise—died due to strangulation."

"We know that now, but my understanding is that wasn't obvious at the time. Milo's parole officer reported he was a model parolee."

"Of course, she did. The PO was also taking bribes from half of the parolees on her watch."

"Again, that came out later."

"How long do you think it would've taken you to find out the parole officer was dirty? Or better yet, wouldn't you have taken the time to investigate the issue? The cops knew Frank wasn't good for the first murder, but they were laser focused on him for the second one. My theory? It was easier to tag him for the crime than it was to prove up the case against Shaw and take down a parole officer, someone who was supposed to be on the side of law and order, in the process. Oh, and did I mention that the parole officer in question happened to be Bruce's partner's sister-in-law? Don't get me wrong, I think there might be a small part of them that actually believed Flynn, the scared, coked-up professor worried his wife would find out he was a cheater and his employer would learn he'd been sleeping with his assistant, was the perfect suspect. They even had cover for not having the DNA tested on the grounds they already knew he'd been sleeping with her, so no news there."

He was right and she knew it, but that didn't make it any easier to accept that her mentor might have been complicit in putting an innocent man away. "Assuming all of this is true, Frank Flynn had an attorney and a full trial. Even if his attorney didn't know there was DNA at the scene, you would think that raising some of the other issues would've been enough to create reasonable doubt."

"He could only bring up the issues he knew about," Nick said.

"A good defense attorney has a duty to thoroughly investigate the case."

"You've met Lionel Darby, haven't you?"

Claire nodded. Lionel was an attorney in private practice who took court appointed cases to bolster his practice. His name was well known in Dallas, mostly because his picture appeared on dozens of billboards, cabs, and bus benches throughout the city. According to courthouse gossip, he'd once been a decent enough attorney, but had a habit of taking on too many clients at once and, as a result, none of them got the attention they deserved. The judges loved to send him court appointments because he never turned one down, which only exacerbated the problem. She'd once been on the witness stand when he'd called his client by the wrong name during cross-examination.

"Granted, Lionel isn't the best, but he wins about as many cases as he loses," she said. "He could've asked the judge for funds to pay an investigator if he wanted to dig deeper. It's an adversarial system. We bring the best evidence we have to the prosecutor, and they do their best with what they've got. Are you saying we're supposed to do the work of the defense attorney too?"

"You know I'm not, but I do think we have to be held to a higher standard. We're in a better position than court appointed attorneys with fewer resources to know things, like about Milo Shaw and the fact his PO was related to one of the detectives who investigated the case. Maybe the relationship didn't have any bearing on why Bruce and his partner didn't look harder at Shaw, but if Lionel had known, he could've made the argument to the jury. All I'm saying is everyone should start with a level playing field, which means having access to the same information. I don't for a minute think you feel any differently."

"I don't, but I'm still not convinced it's up to us to do the leveling. Think about the last time you were on the witness stand. Were you volunteering answers to questions you weren't asked?" She heard the edge in her voice and decided they needed a break from this conversation. "Let's agree to disagree on this one for now." She set her fork down and tossed her napkin on the table. "Where's the next interview?"

"LBJ and the Tollway. Some medical office. I called and told them we'd be there around five," he said.

She did a quick mental calculation. "I've got to take care of something first. I'll drop you by the station and meet you there."

He looked like he wanted to ask why, but decided against it, which saved her from having to make up an excuse. She'd go talk to Riley, and then she could get her head straight and focus on the work they needed to do to catch this killer before they struck again.

Friday afternoon, Riley stepped into the gallery and immediately noticed Lacy was with a customer, so she took a few minutes to look around at the art on display. The upcoming show featured iron sculptures by an artist from Austin, and the gallery had several pieces prominently placed in the main room to tease the opening. She'd seen ads on the side of the McKinney Avenue trolleys for both that show and hers, and she'd heard a snippet on the local NPR station about each on the radio on the way over. She'd chosen the Lofton Gallery not only for their artistic sense, but also their savvy marketing, and her choice was turning out to be a good one.

Lacy spotted her and smiled, holding up a finger to let her know she'd be just a minute. Riley moved on to the second room to survey some of the other pieces on display. One particular sculpture, a tall open hand, struck her with its stark simplicity and realism. It seemed so real, she almost reached out to touch the palm.

"I love when I can see a piece of art and know exactly what it is, don't you agree?"

Riley dropped her hand and turned toward the sound of the familiar voice. She was face-to-face with Claire Hanlon, the last person she expected to see here, but she was glad to see a familiar face. "I'd say I was surprised to see you, but I must be getting used to you popping up in the least expected places."

Claire looked back over her shoulder. "Is there somewhere we can go to talk?"

"Here's fine. The only other person here is the gallery owner and she's busy with a customer. What do you need?"

"After we had dinner, where did you go? What time did you get home?"

Riley scanned Claire's face, looking for a clue as to why she was asking these questions, and with such urgency. The pleasant feeling she'd had upon seeing Claire again started to fade, and her preservation instincts kicked in. "Why?"

"Because I need to know."

Claire's tone wasn't that of a cop engaged in interrogation, it was more like pleading desperation, and Riley's resolve faltered for a moment. The truth was what it was, and she had nothing to hide. "I went back downtown and picked up a few things I'd left on campus. I walked down to the Eye and did a few moonlight sketches because the light was fantastic, unlike this rain today. I don't remember what time I got home, but it was late." She watched Claire's face screw into a painful expression as she spoke. "What's going on?"

"Nothing." Claire's voice was clipped and brisk.

"I can tell it's not nothing." Riley waited a beat while she pondered Claire's questions. At first, she'd mistaken them for genuine interest, but now that she replayed them in her head, they sounded suspiciously like alibi questions. "Wait," she whispered, "you found another body, didn't you?"

"When's the last time you saw your father?"

Oh, no. Now she was crossing the line. "I have answered any questions you've asked, but I will not discuss my father."

"You might want to reconsider that position."

"I think you should leave."

Claire's face was iron. "It's a public place."

"Great, then I'll leave." Riley took a step back, anxious to get away from Claire's watchful gaze and distracting beauty, in order to think things through. She knew without a doubt, the police had found another body. Did they suspect Frank for these murders? Did they suspect her? She couldn't fathom why, but if Frank had done fifteen years for a crime he didn't commit, anything was possible. She took another step back, but this time, Claire reached out and touched her arm.

"I'm sorry. I didn't mean to come on like that."

"Like the hard-assed, suspicious cop you are?"

"I'm only doing my job."

"If you think I could have anything to do with a murder, you're not doing it well. Seriously, I get why you might want to question me and the rest of the club about the murder in Deep Ellum since we were there right before it happened, but now something else has happened and you show up here and start asking me questions like I'm a suspect? What's the connection?"

Claire's face twisted into a pained expression. "I can't tell you."

"Then I have nothing more to say to you." Riley pointed to the exit. "Either you go or I will."

Claire shook her head and started walking to the door. Riley stared at her back, willing her to leave, but also wishing she could catch a glimpse of the woman with whom she'd shared a meal last night. Too late. She was convinced their comfortable dinner had all been an act designed to get her to open up. But for what reason? Were they trying to pin these murders on her father?

"Hey," she called out.

Claire turned. "Yes?"

"How did you know I would be here?"

Claire pulled in her bottom lip like she was considering whether to answer. Finally, she said, "I went by your place to talk to you, but you were in the parking lot getting into your car. I followed you here."

"Why?" Riley genuinely wanted to know, but after a few seconds ticked by without a response, she knew Claire wasn't going to give her the satisfaction of an answer. "Okay, let's see if you'll answer this. If my last name weren't Flynn, would you be following me around?"

For a brief moment, she thought she registered a flicker of regret on Claire's face, but it was gone before she could analyze what it meant. Claire ducked her head and took the last few steps to the door, leaving Riley to her thoughts.

"Is everything okay?" Lacy asked, putting a hand on her arm, much the same way Claire had. "Was that a customer?"

Riley tore her gaze away from the door Claire had exited and looked at Lacy's hand for a moment before lifting her gaze to meet her eyes. "Everything's fine. She was looking for someone, but she was in the wrong place."

Lacy nodded, seemingly satisfied with the answer, and slowly withdrew her hand. "Happens all the time since we moved to this location. Are you ready to go over the new installation details?"

What she wanted to do was follow Claire and demand answers. Why was Claire singularly focused on her when it came to these murders? She made a mental note to check with Buster to see if any of the other members of the sketch club were receiving similar attention, but she figured she already knew the answer. Unless their names were Flynn, they were likely being left alone. Right now, in this moment, she had two choices—obsess about things she couldn't control or focus on her future success. She took a deep breath and slowly let it out, willing the anxiety Claire's visit had delivered to be gone. "Yes, I'm ready."

Now, if she could only get Claire out of her head, she might be able to concentrate on whatever Lacy had in mind.

CHAPTER NINE

Riley drove the short distance from the gallery to the Ginger Man, noting the change in the weather. Yesterday it had been rainy and cold, and now sunny skies and sixty-degree temps beckoned her to be outside sketching. She hoped the nice weather would hold until next Saturday when the sketch club met again.

Buster was waiting at the bar when Riley walked in, and he raised two pints of beer in the air. "'Bout time. I was going to have to drink both of these myself."

Riley took one of the pints and slid into the seat next to him. "I'm thinking you could've handled it." She took a deep drink from the glass and set it down on the bar. Now that she was here, she wasn't sure how to broach the subject she'd come to discuss. She'd planned to ask him if any of the other members of the sketch club had been approached by the police, but if he asked why she wanted to know, she wasn't sure how much she was willing to share.

She took another drink of her beer and decided she was overthinking the topic. "Remember when those cops were in here, wanting to talk to everyone who was in Deep Ellum the day they found that woman who was killed down there?"

"Sure." Buster pointed to the booth in the corner of the bar. "We were over there with Natalie."

"Right. Do you know who else they talked to? Besides us, I mean."

"I gave them a list of everyone in the club, and I told them who was in Deep Ellum with us that day, but I haven't talked to them since." Buster cocked his head. "What's going on?"

"Nothing," she answered quickly. Too quickly judging by the dubious look on his face. She spent a second judging how much she had to share to keep him from digging deeper, and then abandoned all strategy in favor of being able to tell someone what she was going through. "I don't know if I should tell you this."

"Trust me, you should. I can see something's bothering you."

"You can't tell anyone. Not even Natalie."

He drew his hand across his heart. "Swear."

"I think they think I was involved in the murder or that my father was. They say they're talking to everyone who was down by the mural that night, but I'm not sure that's true. And now, I think they've found another body, but I don't know any details, so I don't know if it has anything to do with the first one, but Detective Hanlon followed me around today, and…" She stopped when she noticed Buster's eyes widening. "Sorry. Too much, right?"

"All at once, yes. Let's back up a sec. Why would they think you were involved?"

"Well, I was the last one of us at the mural the night Jill Shasta's body showed up."

"Sounds pretty lame to me," Buster said.

"Agreed." Riley hesitated for a minute, unsure if she really wanted to dive into the subject of her father, but she'd already mentioned him, so she took the plunge. "I don't know if you've been keeping up with the news, but my father is Frank Flynn. He was tried and convicted fifteen years ago, but his conviction was overturned, and he was released from prison last month."

"Whoa."

"Whoa is an understatement," Riley said.

"I bet. Yes, I've been following that story. But he didn't do it, right?"

"Yes. I mean, the court found there were definite problems with the way the case was handled, plus when they finally tested the DNA, it came back as belonging to another guy. The DA's office has supposedly decided not to try him again, but the judge hasn't made a decision about whether to declare him actually innocent. It's all pretty complicated, but the upshot is he's free for now."

"And then a body shows up that makes it look like he might have been involved." Buster took a drink from his beer. "But I don't get why they'd be questioning you about it."

"Me neither. I mean I was down there that day, but like you said, that's a pretty lame connection. I get the impression from talking to the detective that there might be some other murder they are linking to Shasta's death, but I don't have more details, so I can't really defend myself."

"Hard question—do you think your dad could be involved?"

"The truth? I have no idea. Do I want to believe that the man who taught me to ride a bike is a cold-blooded murderer? Absolutely not, but I gave up believing I know this guy years ago. A year or so before he was arrested, he had some kind of premature midlife crisis. He started screwing his much younger teaching assistant and doing coke. Now, he seems sober and he's acting like a model husband, but I don't know him anymore, and after all these years without a father, I'm not sure I want to."

She looked down at her hands where she'd torn the coaster into tiny shreds. "I'm on the verge of getting my big break and I don't need this distraction." The topic of distractions brought to mind Claire's penetrating blue eyes, staring into hers, when they'd shared dinner at Mia's and when Claire had confronted her at the gallery earlier. Claire might be the enemy, but Riley couldn't stop thinking about her, and wishing they'd met under different circumstances. But they hadn't and Claire Hanlon, the detective, was a danger zone, from which she needed to steer clear.

"What can I do?" Buster asked.

She pushed thoughts of Claire away. "I don't know. I guess I just needed to tell someone what was happening. Someone who wouldn't judge me for who my father is."

"No judgment here. Ever." Buster paused for a moment. "I could reach out to everyone on the list I gave them and see if they've talked to the cops. Maybe they'd have some insights about the direction of their investigation."

Riley wanted to say yes because information was power, and right now, she needed to feel like she had some. But she knew this wasn't just about her. "No, don't. The cops might think you're trying to obstruct their investigation. I know I didn't have anything to do with the murder, and if my father did, then he's going to have to deal with the consequences of his actions all on his own. It helped just to talk to you."

"Anytime, pal."

They talked for a bit about her upcoming show, and Riley noted that Buster seemed relieved they'd switched topics. She could hardly blame him, and she couldn't help but wonder if he viewed her differently now that he knew she was related to an accused murderer. As relieved as she'd been to share her story with him, the telling left her feeling awkward and vulnerable, on edge as she waited for the inevitable questions about what life had been like with her father in prison or now that he was newly released. Each time she had to answer, the words chipped away at the self-esteem she'd built on her own all these years. It was time for the cycle to stop. She refused to be defined by the actions of her father, and the next time she saw Claire Hanlon, she was going to tell her so in no uncertain terms.

Claire pulled up in front of her parents' house and parked by the curb since the driveway was already full. The sun had almost set, but she could see enough of the outside of the house to notice the debris sticking out of the gutters and tree branches scraping the roof. She balanced two packages in her arms and walked to the door, noting a few other items in disrepair. The door opened as she approached, and her big brother, Ralph, greeted her with a big smile while he took the packages from her.

"About time you showed up. We've been holding dinner and I'm about to pass out."

"As if." She poked a finger at his broad shoulder. "If you didn't work out so much, maybe you wouldn't be hungry all the time."

"And then I wouldn't be such a catch," he said.

"Who's a catch?"

They both turned to see Ralph's wife, Pia, standing with her hands on her hips. Claire knew her frown wasn't real. "Ralph fancies himself to be quite the stud. You should probably chain him up at home."

"Or let him run free until he gets it out of his system," Pia said. "I could certainly use a break."

Ralph cleared his throat. "Uh, I'm standing right here."

Claire and Pia laughed. "Exactly," Claire said. "Stop talking smack, and we'll leave you alone. Now, what's for dinner and where's the birthday guy?"

"He's in the kitchen," Pia said. She locked arms with Claire, and they headed that way. When they walked into the room, Claire spotted her dad sitting in the breakfast nook. He smiled as she approached, but Claire was certain she spotted a flicker of pain in his eyes when he pushed up from his chair to give her a hug. Today was his sixty-fifth birthday, but he was moving like someone ten years older.

"If it isn't my favorite daughter," he said, keeping up the running joke since Claire was their only daughter. "The detective."

Ralph, the football coach, shook his head. They both knew their dad loved them equally, but Claire was the baby and she'd been spoiled since the day she was born. That she was the only child who'd chosen to wear a uniform, even if it wasn't military, gave her added esteem in her father's eyes. "Oh, Dad, Ralph does the best he can," she said. She raised her nose in the air. "Smells like lasagna." She sniffed again. "And garlic bread. Where's Mom?"

"Right here," her mother said, walking into the kitchen. "Everything's set up in the dining room, and now that we're all here, let's eat."

Claire gave her mother a hug. "Be there in two secs. Just going to go wash my hands." As she left the room, she mouthed to Ralph to follow her, but instead of heading to the bathroom, she detoured to the den.

"What's up, sis?" he asked.

"Does Dad look okay to you?"

"Well, he is a year older," Ralph said with a grin. "Seriously, what's on your mind?"

She paused for a moment and examined whether she was overreacting to her observations before deciding that it was better to mention her concerns than tuck them away. "He seems like he's in some pain, and when I drove up it just looks like he's not keeping the house up the way he used to."

"You know, Pia mentioned that too. The gutters, the trees. The fence gate on the right side of the house is leaning pretty bad too." Ralph frowned. "I was over here last week. I should've noticed."

Claire play punched him in the shoulder. "I'm a detective. It's what I do."

"I'll get over here this week and take care of this stuff and the lawn."

"Hey," she said. "It's not all on you. I'm pretty swamped right now, but I can send over a lawn service to take care of the gutters, trees, and lawn. You fix the fence and check to see if there's anything else that could use your handy touch. We'll tell him the extra attention is part of his birthday present."

"Deal." He glanced back over his shoulder. "We better get in there before Mom decides we don't get any lasagna."

While they ate dinner, they all shared fun birthday memories. The Batman cake her mother had attempted for Ralph's tenth birthday that looked more like a black cat than a superhero, or the surprise party fail when the friend who was assigned to get Claire to her sixteenth birthday party lost track of her at the mall when Claire wandered off to flirt with the redhead who worked at the soft pretzel stand. As they shared stories and laughter, Claire wondered what it would be like to grow up as Riley had, with her father completely out of the picture during her high school years but overshadowing it all with his trial and prison sentence. She couldn't even imagine, and she gave a silent prayer of thanks she didn't have to.

After dinner and presents, Claire leaned over to her father and asked for a moment alone. They walked back to his study, and he invited her to sit on the small sofa across from his desk.

"I could tell something was up when you came in the house," he said, walking over to the liquor cart near his desk. "Scotch?"

A drink would take the edge off, and for a moment, she imagined indulging in the sensation of the amber liquid warming her insides and mellowing the anxiety brewing about the second body, about Riley Flynn, and about how her future rode on solving this case before it got out of hand. But the fix would be temporary, and it would dull her senses. She needed to remain sharp if she was going to solve this case.

"I see what you're doing," her dad said. He poured two glasses, one with three fingers of Scotch and one with half that. He handed her the smaller dose. "A touch won't kill you, and it might be enough to put the voices at bay long enough to focus on what matters."

"How do you always know what I need?"

"Because I've been where you are. In the middle of a case, unable to think of anything else, but having to balance the demands of daily life with those of the job." He tilted his glass toward hers for a toast. "Thanks for making time for us tonight. I appreciate you being here, although I would've understood if you couldn't make it. Your mother, on the other hand. Well, she thinks the whole family has to get together for every birthday." He sighed. "She keeps me grounded. Lord knows, if it wasn't for her, I might've worked twenty-four seven when you and your brother were growing up."

"I get it. The compulsion to keep going until you find the answers. It's not a weakness." Claire drank a sip of the Scotch, instantly warming to the burn. "I have a chance at a big promotion. Squad commander."

Her dad raised his glass. "Something proper to toast. Congratulations."

"It hinges on solving the case I'm working on."

"The girl they found in Deep Ellum."

She resisted correcting the word "girl." "Yes, but there's been another. The manner of death isn't public yet, but it probably will be soon. Another woman, Wendy Hyatt, same MO. Her body was found by one of the bridges downtown."

"Serial killer?"

"Officially, it's too soon to tell, but I'd bet all the money in all the land it is. Too many details about both crime scenes were similar and well planned."

"Any clues?"

"Yes, but they don't make sense." She told him about the drawings, about Riley and Riley's father. About Bruce's obsession with putting Frank Flynn back behind bars. "I get why he's focused on him, but why would Flynn commit a series of murders and leave a clue that led to his daughter. It doesn't make sense."

"You're right. It doesn't." Her dad frowned. "I love Bruce like a brother, but that doesn't mean I think he's always right. Don't let his baggage about the Flynn case weigh down your investigation. If there's a promotion to be had, you'll earn it the right way, not by cutting corners because someone higher up the chain can't see the forest for the trees."

Claire knew his advice was sound, but she couldn't deny the power Bruce had over her career. Her father had retired as a field agent, never having had an interest in moving into administration at the DEA. While she admired his long years of service, she recognized that he didn't get her desire to move up the chain of command any more than she understood why he would be content to take orders rather than give them. If she was going to be in Bruce's position one day, she had to do her time under his control, but Dad was right when he said she didn't have to cut corners, and she took his advice seriously.

"You're right. I'll figure out a way to balance what he wants with my own style." She debated asking another question for a second before plunging ahead. "You don't think Bruce had anything to do with the issues in Frank Flynn's case, do you?"

He laughed. "You'd make a good defense attorney the way you ask leading questions." He set his glass down and crossed his arms. "Look, we've all been in a position where we have a chance to put a finger on the scale to get it to tip in one direction or another. Sometimes, you're absolutely sure giving a nudge in the right direction is necessary to ensure justice is done, but if I've learned anything in all my years doing this it's that if something is right, the truth will bear out, no nudging necessary. All nudging does is rush things along, and rushing might get you where you want to go faster, but you might also lose ground along the way. Understood?"

Claire nodded while mulling over his answer. While not directly implicating Bruce in Flynn's overturned conviction, he was definitely implying it could've happened and it shouldn't have, along with the subtle warning to keep her own counsel when it came to Bruce. "Understood."

"You'll do the right thing," he said. "You always do."

Later, when she'd settled in at home with a glass of wine, she replayed his words. She did try to always do the right thing, but the key was knowing what that was. Her gut told her Riley was not responsible for these murders, but Bruce wanted her to focus her efforts on Riley and her father. It might be time to pay a visit to Frank Flynn so she could get a feel for whether he was an innocent man who'd been in the wrong place at the wrong time or an opportunist who'd cleverly managed to get away with a murder and was out committing more. Contacting Frank would be delicate. He was probably represented by counsel for his appeal, so she would have to be careful not to ask him questions about that case, but even if all she got was a chance to judge his reaction to questions about these recent murders, it would be worth it to talk to him. She sent Nick a text suggesting they pay Frank a visit the next day.

She set the phone down and stared at the few drops left in her glass of wine while she tried to decide if she should go to bed or have another glass. Right now, she was too agitated for sleep. She should be doing something to try to solve this case, but it was late and, other than sitting on the couch reviewing the evidence over and over, her options were limited. She stood to get another glass of wine, and that's when the idea came to her. On the way to the kitchen, she stopped at her laptop on the bar and ran a few quick searches. When she was done, she picked up her phone, dialed dispatch, and requested the watch commander.

"This is Detective Hanlon. I need a patrol unit assigned to the following two addresses until further notice." She rattled off the info while she poured another modest glass of the Pinot. "Have them call me before they go out. I have special instructions."

She didn't have the authority on her own to request full-scale surveillance of Riley and her father, but having someone watch the house and report back on their comings and goings would be enough to narrow her focus for now, and the extra step should show Bruce she was taking his admonition to focus her investigation on the Flynns seriously. Plus, she had to admit she wouldn't mind focusing more attention on Riley, but that desire had little to do with the murder investigation and everything to do with feelings she shouldn't have.

Chapter Ten

Riley reread the article in the *Dallas Morning News* for the third time over her Monday morning tea. She didn't usually read the news, having been cured of curiosity about current events by the onslaught of media during her father's trial, but a nagging suspicion that Claire had been holding something back about the Shasta case led her to the internet to see what she could find.

A few quick searches led her to this story about a dead body found by a runner on Friday morning near the Margaret Hunt Hill Bridge. The deceased, Wendy Hyatt, a twenty-three-year-old white female, had been employed as a paralegal at a downtown law firm, and before her body had been found, she'd last been seen working late on Thursday evening. Preliminary cause of death—strangulation. At the very end of the copy there was a brief mention of Jill Shasta. The reporter had contacted the police department spokesperson to determine if there were similarities between the two cases but had been told the department wouldn't comment on an ongoing investigation. Riley wasn't an expert on criminal justice, but she knew enough to know the official statement was code for probably, and we know a helluva lot more, but we're not ready to tell you yet.

Claire's question about when she'd last seen her father echoed in her head as it had for the last two days. She hadn't answered out of pure stubbornness, but what if Claire had a legitimate reason for wanting to know? Riley didn't know much about what her dad had been up to since he'd been released, other than reconnecting with her mother and trying to wind his way back into her life. She remembered his offer to let her talk to his attorney about his case. Had the gesture been made out of confidence or did he think she might not take him up on it? Was he a possible suspect in the deaths of these young women, or was Claire simply trying to provoke a reaction, and if so, why?

Riley spent another half hour looking for more details about the murders, but the vague statement from DPD was the only news on the subject. Annoyed that the internet consisted of nothing more than a spinning wheel of information, packaged differently, but still the same, she turned off her laptop and poured another cup of tea, while she contemplated the day ahead. Other than preparing a few sketches for Lacy, her late afternoon watercolor class was the only thing on her agenda. She reached for her wallet lying on the table and fished out the card Claire had given her when she and her partner had come here last week. When she turned it over, she found Claire's cell phone on the back. Before she could overthink her impulse, she picked up her phone and dialed.

"Hanlon here."

The sound of Claire's sharp and sure voice caused Riley to have second thoughts. She started to disconnect the call, ready to explain she'd dialed by accident if confronted on the subject.

"Can I help you?"

Riley paused at the question. Police were supposed to be the helpful ones, the heroes, an alleged fact she'd learned in kindergarten through picture books and admonitions that they were the people you run to when you're in trouble. Other than the past week, she'd only had the experience of them ripping her father from their home, apparently without cause, to convince her otherwise. Frank's arrest had been a giant, life-altering experience for sure, but she was savvy enough to know that there were plenty of good things law enforcement did. If her father was a murderer, it was the cops' job to put him back in prison, but was it up to her to help them? The dilemma tied her brain in knots, but she did what she knew how to do best and went with her gut. "Maybe. It's Riley. Riley Flynn."

"Good to hear from you," Claire said, a hint of surprise in her voice.

"I didn't expect to be calling."

"But you did."

Riley gripped the phone. In a minute, Claire was going to ask why. What would she tell her when she wasn't even sure of her motive? She settled on a question to buy time. "Meet me for an early lunch?"

A brief pause, then Claire said, "Just a sec."

Her response was Riley's first indication Claire was taken off guard, and it gave her a slight feeling of satisfaction. Riley heard muffled voices, and a few moments later, Claire came back on the line.

"Lunch sounds great. Where?"

"Mia's. Eleven thirty. See you there." Riley hung up before Claire could reply. She'd picked Mia's because it was her territory, so she could be comfortable, but she felt nothing but discomfort at the idea of meeting Claire without setting clear parameters in advance. She stared at the phone, trying to decide if she should send a text to cancel, but her own curiosity won out. She could handle this.

The hostess at Mia's greeted her with a broad smile. "Hello, Riley." She plunked a single menu from the stand. "Follow me."

"Actually, I'm meeting someone here. Tall, blond, looks like a cop." She cracked a grin, ready to explain, but Claire walked through the door at that moment, saving her from having to articulate a description, which was good, because no description could adequately describe Claire's perfectly put together beauty and confident bearing. She was dressed in a sharply tailored black suit like the one she'd worn to the funeral, and it struck Riley that, dressed as she was, Claire looked more like a corporate VP than a cop. "Here she is."

The hostess looked at Claire like she was sizing her up and then gave Riley an approving smile. "Right this way."

The waiter, Daniel, was at their table right away and he gave Riley a thumbs-up behind Claire's back. Apparently, while she'd been enjoying dining alone all these years, everyone here thought she needed to be coupled up. Boy, were they misreading the situation. She could definitely admit Claire was extremely attractive, and maybe, under other circumstances, she'd consider asking Claire out, but things would fall apart around the third or fourth date, like they always did when she wouldn't open up and share more about her personal life, dodging questions about her family.

Except Claire already knew who her father was. Riley couldn't decide if her knowing made things better or worse.

After they ordered a repeat of the meal they'd shared the week before, Claire was the first to speak. "I was surprised you called."

"I could tell. I decided if you're going to follow me around anyway, we may as well meet somewhere where we can actually talk. Ambushing me at the gallery wasn't cool."

"True. It was impulsive, not my normal style." Claire reached for the chips and salsa. "These are the best chips in Dallas," she said, and dug in as if to curtail any further conversation on the point.

Riley filed the interesting nugget of information and acted on an impulse of her own. "Was your impulse spurred by the second dead body? The one from Friday morning? Do you think the murders were committed by the same person?"

Claire took her time chewing the bite in her mouth. When she finally replied, she said, "Officially, I can't comment."

"Good thing I'm not official."

Riley waited through the long pause that followed and watched the subtle changes in the expression on Claire's face. A moment ago, digging into the salsa and chips, she'd been smiling in pleasure, but her face lost all affect the minute she said the word "officially." Now, she looked simply frustrated. Riley resisted the urge to say anything else for fear she'd tip the balance away from obtaining any information about the case.

"We think the cases are related, but I can't tell you why."

"So, there's some reason besides the fact both women were white, in their twenties, and strangled?" Riley didn't bother trying to hide the sarcasm in her voice.

"Someone's been doing their research."

"I read the paper. I'd hardly call that research. You can't really think I'm involved in these murders, can you?"

"Everyone's a suspect, until they aren't."

"Do you even hear yourself? If you have an accusation to make, go ahead and tell me what it is and I'll tell you why you're wrong. That is unless you've already made up your mind."

Claire looked frustrated again, and a long beat passed before she spoke, this time to change the subject entirely. "The painting of the Eye at your apartment was stunning. Tell me about your process."

Riley wanted to answer with her own question about why Claire had wanted to know, but instead she decided to play along in hopes that answering Claire might be repaid by answers to her own questions. "I spend a lot of time sketching before I ever start painting, with oils anyway. I often use watercolors when I'm out with the group."

"When did you first join the Eastside Sketchers?"

"A couple of years ago." Riley grinned at the memory. "It was kind of an accident. I was at White Rock Lake one Saturday afternoon, sketching the sailboats when Buster and about eight other people showed up with their sketchbooks and easels. They set up next to me and we started talking. When they left a couple of hours later, Buster told me the site of their next meeting and invited me to join them. I've joined them every other Saturday since."

"Buster seems like a nice guy."

"He is, and he's incredibly talented. He's the one who connected me to the Lofton Gallery. I'm lucky he's taken an interest in my career." Riley immediately wished she hadn't shared her personal feelings, but Claire's obvious and intense interest in something other than her father had drawn her out.

She was saved from saying more when Daniel appeared with their food. They tucked into the tacos and spent the rest of the meal talking about the innocuous topic of food and their favorite Tex-Mex restaurants around the city, but when Daniel returned to clear their empty plates, Claire launched back into her questions. "Why isn't any of your artwork online?"

Riley shrugged. "Why would it be?"

"Google any artist and they've got samples of their work on the web, either showing it for sale or on social media to promote their work. Most of the people in your sketch group post their drawings, and they're amateurs."

"Maybe it's because they're amateurs. They have nothing to lose by putting their work up for the whole world to criticize and copy. I get that everyone thinks they have to put their entire lives on the internet in some ironic quest to be authentic, but that's not me. I've spent years building a portfolio, so I could get representation. Other than the dean at Richards, no one has seen my work before I submitted it to the Lofton. If I were starting out trying to get licensed on a large scale, I imagine social media stats would be important, but Lacy Lofton likes the idea that they are rolling out a debut of never before seen artwork. I'm sure there'll be plenty of promotion on social media after the show." It suddenly struck her that Claire had been scouring the internet for information about her art. "Why the interest in my work?"

Claire shifted in her seat and developed a sudden fascinating interest in the last remaining bits of chips and salsa. "Just curious."

Riley knew there was some other reason, but she sensed pushing the point wouldn't get her anywhere. "Okay."

"How long have you been teaching?"

Happy to have a change in subject, Riley answered easily. "Three years. I did the usual starving artist thing after college, working in art supply stores and applying to galleries and museums. One of my professors at Richards told me about a continuing ed class they offered. The instructor that was lined up to teach the class quit suddenly and they needed someone to fill in. I took the gig and it eventually led to teaching classes for credit. I'm an adjunct, which allows me the freedom to go off and do my own thing when I'm not teaching, but the pay is pretty crappy."

"You must do okay," Claire said. "I mean you live in a great part of town. That brownstone can't be cheap."

Riley heard the underlying meaning—she wasn't successful enough at anything to deserve to live where she did. The implication stung. "If you have a question, ask it."

"Maybe you have a roommate who helps pay the bills."

"Maybe you spend too much time talking to criminals to get how rude you sound when you talk to regular people. I don't have a roommate. Not that it's any of your business, but I have a deal with the building owner. I'm the on-site super. I can't do anything fancy, but I can handle simple plumbing repairs, a stuck door, or minor electrical work, like changing out a light switch. I'm on call for repairs and emergencies, and in exchange I get a great deal on the rent. That's not illegal is it?" She hadn't meant to get angry, but the more she thought about the question, the more it pissed her off. "Where do *you* live and how do you pay for it?"

"I'm sorry." Claire offered a tentative smile. "Nosiness is an occupational hazard."

Riley stared into her eyes, looking for a sign Claire's questions were more personal than professional, but she wasn't ready to trust her instincts where Claire was concerned. Already, she'd talked more during this lunch than she ever had while sharing a meal with another attractive woman. For a short while, she'd almost forgotten Claire was a cop and any questions she asked weren't asked out of a friendly desire to know, but rather to catch a killer. Which brought her back to the question Claire wouldn't answer: why was she so interested in her artwork?

She'd have to figure that out on her own, but in the meantime, it was time to bring the conversation around to the reason she'd wanted to meet Claire today. "Speaking of nosy. You've asked about my father. Do you think he's involved in these murders?"

If Claire was shocked at the blunt question, she didn't show it. She did glance around as if to ensure no one was listening in, and she lowered her voice. "I don't know. Do you think he is?"

Riley's instinct was to shut this conversation down, but she paused and put herself in Claire's place, starting with the premise everyone was a suspect. Her approach was abhorrent when it came to people who should be above suspicion, but Riley knew the fact Frank had been in the system would be a forever taint to his reputation no matter what a judge might say about his innocence. Still, it wasn't fair. "You don't think he should've been released, do you?"

"What?"

"You're one of those cops who thinks that just because someone gets convicted on a technicality, they still deserve what's coming to them."

"I don't appreciate being lumped in with anyone. I have my own mind and I make my own decisions based on the evidence I find."

"Do you think my father was guilty of killing Linda Bradshaw?"

"I don't know. I didn't sit through the trial, hear what the jury heard."

"The jury apparently didn't hear everything," Riley said.

"That's for a judge to decide."

"Kind of a chickenshit answer, don't you think?"

"It's the only answer I have. I know what you know. Do *you* believe he was guilty?"

Riley wished the answer wasn't such a struggle. She'd been wrestling with this question since the day the detectives had arrested her father. The words came out before she could stop them. "I don't know." She looked down and saw that she'd torn her napkin into tiny little pieces and she shoved the debris to the side. “But it doesn’t really matter what I think. His case was mishandled, depriving him of a fair trial.”

“Some people think the best way to resolve a situation like that is with a new trial,” Claire said.

“And by some people, you mean cop people, right?” Riley shook her head. “He did fifteen years. If he’s tried again and found not guilty, what’s the remedy then?”

“I don’t know.” Claire grimaced. “The system isn’t perfect, but it works most of the time.”

Riley let the statement go without comment. She could hardly expect to influence Claire when she wasn’t certain of the facts. Deep down, she didn’t believe her father was guilty of murder, but she wasn’t equipped to argue the finer legal points. She was, however, determined to find out why Claire was considering him a suspect in these recent murders. “Tell me what other clues you have in these recent murders. You keep coming back to me about them. Maybe if you give me a clue what you’re looking for, I can help you.”

“We’re looking at lots of things, people.”

“Like who?” Riley wanted Claire to either admit she was a suspect and tell her why or move on. She pressed the point. “Do you think I was involved?”

A slight pause and then Claire said, “We are covering a lot of ground and it’s too soon for me to comment on the status of a pending investigation.”

“What a nicely packaged bullshit answer. Are you really looking at a lot of possible suspects? Because it seems like you’re only focused on ones whose last name is Flynn.”

Claire bit her lower lip. Riley could tell she wanted to respond, but something was keeping her from it, and Riley had lost all patience about the subject. “You really have nothing to say?”

“Riley…”

Riley stood and pushed her chair in. “We’re done here. Don’t contact me again,” she said, feeling silly as she said the words, since she'd been the one to call Claire this time. "I mean it." She tossed a couple of twenties on the table. "And lunch is on me. If you want to know where I got this money, get a subpoena for my bank records."

She stalked off without looking back. When she slid behind the wheel of her SUV, she slammed her palms against the steering wheel to drain some of her anger before she pulled out onto the road. Her anger was directed inward. She'd lapsed into a feeling of comfort, sharing easy conversation with Claire like they were friends, when she should've realized Claire was a cop looking for clues and any questions she asked were to bolster her investigation against the most convenient suspect so she could close this case and move on to the next. She'd let herself believe that Claire was different from the cops who'd arrested her father, who'd settled on the easiest explanation instead of the right one, letting expediency substitute for justice. And she'd done so because Claire was beautiful and engaging and all the things she'd never have because of a life story she did not create.

CHAPTER ELEVEN

Claire sat at the table for a few moments while she tried to process what had just happened. When Riley had called her and offered to meet, she'd taken the overture as an opportunity to see what she could find out about the elusive artist as it related to the case, but when she'd seen Riley again, her instinct to interrogate took a back seat to a genuine desire to get to know her, to see beneath the no affect veneer Riley projected, but now she was as mystified as she'd been from the start.

Did Riley believe her father was innocent or not? Did she? Claire heard Nick's voice in her head, saying she should weigh the facts in light of the issues the detectives caused by withholding evidence. She believed in the importance of loyalty, but if her primary allegiance wasn't to the truth, she wasn't doing her job. Her gut told her Riley didn't have anything to do with these crimes, but truth was based on facts and evidence, not gut feelings.

She should've shown Riley the sketches, asked her outright if they were hers. The second murder meant it was past time to keep the sketches a secret if they wanted to catch the murderer. If Riley said the drawings were hers, they might have enough to get a search warrant for Riley's apartment to see if there was any other evidence to tie her to the case. If she said the drawings weren't, then it was time to show them to the rest of the Eastside Sketchers to see if someone else claimed ownership. Either way, they needed a break and they needed it soon.

Her phone buzzed with a text from Nick. *Reyes wants us to come by. Where are you?*

Oak Lawn, she typed back. *I'll pick you up.*

On the way to the station, Claire considered what she would tell Nick when he asked where she'd been. It wasn't like they were joined at the hip, but she knew he'd have opinions about her sharing a meal with a person of interest in the case and for sure he'd wonder why she was meeting Riley without him. Ultimately, she decided to hope he wouldn't ask—not the most ingenious strategy, but it was the best she could come up with short of outright lying.

She pulled alongside the building and texted Nick she was waiting outside. A few minutes later, he got in the car.

"What's up?" she asked. "Did Reyes give you a clue why she wants to see us?"

"Nope, but you know how she hates the phone when she wants to make a point."

"Accurate." Claire maneuvered her way through traffic to the medical examiner's office, trying to think of something to say that wouldn't provoke a discussion of Riley Flynn or her father. "I keep thinking about Buster Creel. Remember he said he left the rest of the group early the day Jill Shasta was murdered."

"Right, because he had to go let out his dog."

"What if he doubled back and dumped her body while the others were on the way to the bar?"

"I'll have to check my notes," Nick said, "but I think he made it to the bar before Riley."

"He could've taken a different route."

"True, but you saw his work online. Those sketches definitely aren't his. I guess he could've gotten hold of someone else's work, but why would he choose to leave it at the murder scene?"

Claire tapped her fingers on the steering wheel. Nick was right, of course. They'd found samples online of most of the group member's work, but none of them appeared to be the same style as the sketches they'd found at the murder scenes. She was desperately casting about for anything that might clear Riley, and her desperation was a problem since it had the potential to compromise their investigation. "Any luck finding samples of Riley's work?"

"None. I've looked everywhere."

"I think it's time we go to the Lofton Gallery and see if we can convince them to give us a sneak preview of her work."

"I thought you didn't want to tip anyone off."

"I don't, but I'd rather do that than have more dead bodies show up because we're focused on the wrong suspect."

"On it." Nick jabbed at his phone. "Uh, not going to happen today. Gallery's closed. They open back up Thursday at noon."

"Let's be there when they open." Claire had mixed feelings about the decision to strong-arm the gallery. Her gut told her Riley didn't have anything to do with the murders, but she was ready for a break in this case and she could no longer afford to tiptoe around evidence in the name of a strategy that wasn't paying off. She pulled up at the Dallas County Medical Examiner's office, and she and Nick went in and asked for Dr. Sophia Reyes.

A few minutes later, Reyes appeared in the lobby and motioned for them to follow her back to her office. "You two look like shit."

"Thanks, Doc," Nick said. "Between this case and the four babies my wife delivered over the weekend, I'm not getting much sleep. Medical question for you—why do babies always seem to come in the middle of the night, especially if it's the weekend?"

"You know what they say. The best and worst things happen in the middle of the night. It's definitely when we get the most dead bodies. How about you, Claire? What's your excuse for looking like you slept on a bed of nails?"

"Same. Except the part about the babies." Claire kept her answer simple, but she knew it wasn't. Unlike Nick, she'd had uninterrupted time in the middle of the night, but sleep eluded her. In its place was a constant stream of unanswered questions and jumbled emotions, most of which revolved around Riley Flynn. "What've you got for us?"

Reye's handed her a file. "Tox screen and fiber analysis. I had to rush these along, so consider the results preliminary, but there are a few interesting items."

Claire opened the folder and held it between her and Nick. She scanned the first page. "Tell me what we're looking at." She pointed at a section in the middle of the page. "Because it looks like this says there were GHB levels in each of these women."

"That's correct. The question is whether it was endogenous or exogenous."

"English please," Claire asked.

"She means whether it was introduced into the body or whether the body created it during the decomposition process," Nick said.

"Thanks, nerd man."

He shrugged. "Years of helping Cheryl study. Oh, and I took a couple of forensics courses online last year. Besides, chemistry is my jam."

Claire turned back to Reyes. "Is he right?"

"Essentially, yes. GHB doesn't stay in the bodily fluids for very long, and measuring the exact levels is complicated by regular metabolism and the fact the body's cells can produce GHB during decomposition. There have been studies that look at the measurement parameters to determine which is which, and based on my own research, it's entirely possible these women were drugged. The science around this is complicated though, and a good defense expert will be able to challenge my conclusions, but I wanted you to know about it because if these women were given GHB, they likely wouldn't have been able to resist being strangled."

"Which widens the pool of possible suspects to anyone who could drug a drink," Nick said.

"Whoever it was would've still had to find an opportunity to administer the GHB, so either they were able to get close enough to slip it in a drink or they overpowered them to administer the drug, and if it's the latter, then why bother with the drug if you're already in a struggle." Claire stared at the page. "What about DNA? Anything showing a defensive struggle?"

"No," said Reyes. "And the GHB would explain why. If he drugged the women, they wouldn't have been able to resist."

"Or she," said Nick. "We don't know if the perp is a he or a she, yet, and if whoever it was used a drug to debilitate the victims, it would've been easy to strangle them."

Claire's stomach roiled at the word "she." She couldn't imagine the Riley she'd shared civil conversation and brisket tacos with dosing an unsuspecting woman and then strangling her to death, but any questions about whether Riley had the strength to do so were laid to rest by this new finding. "You said you had some info on the fibers?"

"Yes." Reyes took the file and flipped to another page. "We found some trace fibers on the neck of each woman and were able to match them to the same material. Silk. We don't have the capability here to determine if they were both from the same item, but I took the liberty of sending samples to the FBI lab. "We also found some dog hairs. Did either woman have a dog?"

"No for Shasta. I don't know about Wendy Hyatt," Claire said. "There wasn't one at her apartment. We're meeting with her parents this afternoon and we can ask them." She scrawled a reminder in her notebook. "How soon will you know about the fibers?"

"I put a rush on it, but you know how that goes. Hurry up and wait. It just depends on where we are in line. I'll call you as soon as I know more."

"Thanks. Anything else we need to know?"

"No." Reyes pointed at the folder. "Leave that here. I'll get you a copy of my official report as soon as I hear back from the lab."

Claire thanked her for the heads-up and she and Nick left the building. Once they were in the car, Claire's head was buzzing with ideas. "I'm not sure what to think about all that. Any thoughts?"

"My first thought is Buster Creel has a dog."

"Let's find out what kind." Claire jotted a note as a reminder.

"How about you?" Nick asked. "Did anything else Reyes said give you any revelations?"

"I'd have to look back through the files, but I don't think Frank Flynn strangled Linda Bradshaw with anything other than his bare hands."

"Uh, you seem to be forgetting that he probably didn't strangle anyone at all, but no need to look back through the case file. Linda Bradshaw's killer left handprints not silk fibers. You still think we should talk to him?"

Claire considered her answer carefully. Bruce had texted her this morning to ask where things stood regarding Flynn. His impatience at the stagnant investigation was apparent from the use of all caps on the word FLYNN. She hadn't bothered responding to ask which Flynn he was talking about since she figured he wouldn't care as long as he could tie one of them to the murders. And that was the problem, wasn't it? Bruce cared more about exacting punishment for what he perceived as a missed opportunity in Linda Bradshaw's case, and it felt more like revenge than justice. But his obsession was her problem because Frank Flynn's hearing was coming up, and if she didn't give Bruce something he could use to keep Flynn from being completely exonerated, she could kiss her promotion good-bye. "I think we should at least try."

"I hear he's staying at a place in Oak Cliff."

"He is." She grimaced at his questioning look. "I did a little digging. And I got a squad car assigned to both his place and Riley's. Not full surveillance, just to keep an eye on their comings and goings."

"When were you going to tell me about it?" Nick asked, clearly annoyed.

"There wasn't really a chance. I thought about it last night and didn't know it had been approved until I was on my way to lunch."

"Secret lunch," he said with a grunt. "If you and Bruce are going to work this case together, I'm not sure why I'm here."

She started to protest his characterization of her lunch, but she wasn't ready to tell him she'd shared a meal with Riley, which made it secret after all. "I'm not doing Bruce's bidding, but even if I was, he outranks us both. Don't tell me that if he gave you a direct order you would disobey it."

"I wouldn't, but there's a difference between taking orders and currying favors."

"Wow." Claire couldn't remember Nick ever confronting her like this before and it stung. "Tell me how you really feel."

"I'm looking out for you, like you'd do for me. I know Bruce is your guy in the department, but be careful tying your future to him. If he goes down, you will too."

Claire didn't respond. Nick was right, but his warning was premised on Bruce having done something wrong. All he'd done so far was urge her to look harder at a couple of persons of interest. Any other superior might do the same, and she'd be expected to follow orders, old family friendship or not. No, Bruce wasn't the obstacle here, but her growing attraction to Riley Flynn was definitely a problem, and if she wasn't careful, it could cost her career.

CHAPTER TWELVE

Riley tugged at the sleeves of her blazer to keep the scratchy wool from rubbing against her wrists. She wasn't sure why she'd felt the need to upgrade her clothing for this meeting, but the memory of her mother urging her to put on her Sunday best to go meet with the lawyers was a strong probability.

The offices of Bradley and Casey were located on the south side of downtown, and there was plenty of parking behind the building. As she walked down the block, she remembered a time a couple of months ago when the Eastside Sketchers had met down the street at the old Sears building that was now a mixed-use development called Southside on Lamar. It had started to rain that day and most of the group bugged out when the raindrops started to fall, but she, Buster, Jensen, and Warren had stayed for the full two hours to be rewarded by a blast of sunshine from the fickle Texas sky as they were packing up. She smiled at the memory of them making the most of a bad situation and realized she treasured her time with the group more than she realized.

The next meet-up was Saturday at the Dallas Farmer's Market. She was strongly considering not attending. She would tell Buster it was because she was busy getting ready for her show at the Lofton, but really it was because she associated their last meet-up with Jill Shasta's death. Despite the fact she hadn't witnessed the crime scene, she hadn't been able to get the image of a dead body against the backdrop of the beautiful mural out of her mind. And while she hadn't been at the Margaret Hunt Hill Bridge the day the second body had been found, she'd often sketched the stunning bridge, and one of her paintings of the landmark would be featured at her opening.

It felt like her entire life was on hold since Claire Hanlon had appeared in her life. Normally, she wouldn't be reading the news, but lately she couldn't get enough, digging deep in internet searches to memorize every detail of these deaths while Claire's questions played on a loop in the back of her mind. She didn't care about the questions that implicated her, because she knew she hadn't done anything wrong, but when it came to her father, she couldn't be entirely sure. Which was why she'd taken him up on his offer to meet with the attorney who'd handled his appeal and get the firsthand details about why the conviction had been overturned.

She pushed through the doors of the building and took a look around. The reception area was cozier and more welcoming than she would've expected from a well-known attorney. The attorney who'd represented her father at his trial had been court appointed, and although he had an office, he'd always wanted to meet with them at the courthouse, crammed into one of the rooms for defense attorneys at the back of the courtroom. They'd stood in a corner listening to his summary of the evidence and plea negotiations, her mother asking questions while she kept her mouth shut like a good girl. Later she learned the attorney was court appointed because her father lost his job when he'd been arrested, and he'd already spent their savings on his affair and the drugs he used to be someone else—someone who forgot he had a family to care for. How had he, an inmate of the Texas Department of Corrections, afforded these attorneys with their fancy office?

"Can I help you?"

Riley looked up to see a gorgeous redhead standing a few feet from her, and she wondered how long she'd been standing in the middle of the reception area lost in thought. "I'm here to see Morgan Bradley. My name is Riley Flynn."

The woman smiled and it was full of warmth. She stuck out her hand. "I'm Morgan. It's a pleasure to meet you, Riley." She motioned to a door. "Come on back."

Riley followed her to a beautiful conference room. On the conference room table were stacks of files, in neat rows. "Looks like you're in the middle of a big case."

Morgan chuckled. "Always, but this one is about to be over. These are your father's files. He asked me to give you access to everything and answer any questions you have. I've blocked out some time today, and we can make an appointment for next week after his hearing if you have more questions."

Riley stared at the files, overwhelmed by the amount of material. She wouldn't even know where to begin. "Could we start with a rundown of what next week's hearing is about?"

"Sure." Morgan motioned to one of the chairs. "Have a seat." She waited until Riley was settled. "Hearing is probably not the best word for it since it's unlikely there will be any witnesses for the judge to hear. Basically, we've filed motions asking the judge, in light of the issues with your father's case that led to the conviction being overturned, to declare him actually innocent."

"I'm pretty sure I know the answer to this, but how is that different from having the conviction overturned?"

"In theory, if the conviction is nullified, the DA's office can start over with a new trial and try again because there was essentially no verdict. But if the judge declares him innocent, then jeopardy attaches, and he can't be tried again. Plus, and this hasn't been important to Frank, but he is eligible for a heightened level of compensation for his wrongful incarceration if he's found to have been innocent."

"He'll get money?"

"Yes. It's usually a set amount for the number of years he served."

Riley let the information gel for a moment. "How did he afford to pay you, or is he counting on this money to pay your fees?"

"Our firm took his case pro bono. We take on at least one big appellate case a year in consultation with the Innocence Project. They don't have the resources to handle every case that comes to them, and although our contribution is small, we feel like it's important to do our part."

"You keep saying 'we.'" Riley looked around for reference to who else she might be talking about. "Who else worked with you on my father's case?"

Morgan smiled broadly. "My law partner, Parker Casey. I'd introduce you, but she's in trial this week. Parker was a big help on your father's case. She used to be a homicide detective with the Dallas Police Department, as is the investigator we use, and they are both very familiar with the proper procedures and protocols for handling evidence."

"Parker sounds like a valuable resource."

"She is." Morgan smiled broadly. "She also happens to be my wife, so I can vouch for her personally." She leaned forward and crossed her hands on the table. "I realize that might not mean much to you since you don't know me very well, but feel free to ask around. I have a reputation for getting to the truth, and that's what happened in this case."

"Why didn't his original attorney learn all of this?"

"I don't know. I don't mean to cast aspersions in hindsight, but I can't excuse the fact he didn't dig very deep at all. Unfortunately, there are some attorneys who take on more than they can handle. The court appointed system unwittingly supports that when judges load up attorneys with lots of cases and the attorneys are making so little on each case, they are motivated to take on too much. But it's not entirely his fault. The detectives assigned to the case appear to have actively hidden information from him. It's much harder to get to the truth if you don't know it exists."

"The DNA?"

"Yes."

Riley took a moment to process this information. "What makes a cop do something like that?"

"Good question. And let me be the first to say, I think most police officers are honorable people who risk their lives every day for very little money or recognition. That said, I think we're all motivated by a desire to be right, to find confirmation of our beliefs. These detectives were convinced your father was the killer, and they weren't wrong to look at him as a suspect. Their shortfall was their failure to look beyond their initial beliefs and check their assumptions. If they had, they likely would've found the real killer, but to do so would've resulted in difficulty for one of them."

"The one whose sister-in-law was the parole officer?"

"Right. I think both detectives were at fault here, but when it comes to the more active cover-up, he's the one who had the most to lose."

"You said the hearing would consist primarily of motions. Can I get copies of those?"

Morgan reached toward the closest stack of paper. "I had a feeling you might ask and I've prepared a binder with all of the appeal filings. Most of it is fairly boring legalese, but you'll get the gist." She handed a thick black binder to Riley.

"Thank you. One more question, if you don't mind."

"Not at all."

"What are his chances? Of being declared innocent, I mean?"

"If the DA's office follows through with their decision not to retry the case, I think the judge will take that as a strong signal they do not have a solid case, but it's not a guarantee of innocence. That said, I think the chances are good." Morgan paused. "Do you plan to be at the hearing?"

Riley's skin started to crawl as the memory of being in court for the reading of her father's trial verdict came surging back to her. She'd been in the front row of the courtroom, seated next to her mother, standing directly behind her father when the jury filed back into the courtroom. Even though her father's attorney had said not to read anything from their expressions, their downcast eyes spoke volumes, and she felt her knees lock and her palms grew sweaty. Her father looked back and gave her a comforting smile, reminiscent of a time in her childhood when their relationship was close, but she could see the edge of fear in his eyes and knew he was as worried as she was. She remembered thinking he'd been missing from her life for a while now; why did she suddenly care about the prospect of losing him completely?

"Are you okay?"

Morgan's gentle voice penetrated her thoughts and she shook away the memory. She was an adult now and she'd done without her father for the majority of her life. Whatever happened next week, she could handle it with the same fortitude she'd handled what had come before, but she didn't need to be in the room when it happened. In the meantime, she had her own legal issues.

"Do you know Detective Claire Hanlon?"

"I do," Morgan said. "But she wasn't involved in your father's case. I don't think she was even in the department back then."

"I didn't think so," Riley said, torn between wishing she'd kept her mouth shut and wanting to know everything possible about the woman who had been dogging her every move. She ignored the roaring anxiety that came with wondering about Claire and pressed on. "I guess I'm just curious about your impression of her overall. She's investigating two recent murders. The one from Deep Ellum and the one—"

"By the Margaret Hunt Hill Bridge," Morgan said, finishing her sentence. She cocked her head. "Detective Hanlon is a cop's cop. She is very loyal to the department and is on her way up the ranks from what I hear. Do you mind me asking how you know she's involved in those investigations?"

Riley hesitated, uncomfortable about sharing Claire's fixation with her and her father with a stranger when she hadn't even mentioned it to her father. She'd considered calling him, but every time she got close to picking up the phone, she experienced a sense of dread at the idea of reconnecting over the very kind of thing that had severed their relationship in the first place. *Hey, Dad, Dallas cops think you might be guilty of murder again. Okay, bye.* No matter how many times she played potential scripts, she couldn't see the conversation leading anywhere good. But she could tell Morgan. After all, she'd voluntarily taken on his legal battles. What was one more to add to the list?

"Claire, uh, Detective Hanlon, has asked questions about my father. Whether I think he really killed Linda Bradshaw. Whether I've been in contact with him." She took a breath and realized she needed to give more context. "I'm in an urban sketch group and we were in Deep Ellum at the exact spot where Jill Shasta was discovered earlier that day. Detective Hanlon and her partner have questioned most of us who were there that day, but they—she's—taken a particular interest in me. I don't know if she thinks I'm involved, but I suspect it's because I'm Frank Flynn's daughter."

Morgan asked a few questions and made some notes of every conversation Riley had with Claire about Frank. "Thank you for telling me about this. Have you spoken to your father about it?"

"No, I'll let you handle that. We're not exactly close."

"I imagine fifteen years apart will do that."

"It's more than the span of time. We'd grown apart before he went to prison. He'd changed."

"I get it."

They sat for a few moments in silence, and Riley appreciated that Morgan didn't feed her a bunch of platitudes about how he might be different now. "I should probably go."

"What are you going to do about Detective Hanlon?"

"What do you mean?"

"I mean if she's got her sights on you for this case, she's not likely to let go."

"I'm not worried. I don't have anything to hide."

"Said half the people who hire me," Morgan said. "Trust me. Claire Hanlon is tenacious. You're better off not talking to her at all." Morgan handed her a business card. "If she contacts you again, tell her you'd be happy to talk to her, but to go through me. I'll get her off your back."

Riley stared at the card in Morgan's hand, tempted to turn it down, but she took it out of courtesy. "I should get going. I have a class to teach this afternoon." She stood to leave.

"Art class?" At Riley's surprised look, Morgan added, "Your dad mentioned you are a very talented artist and that you're teaching at Richards College."

"It pays the bills until I make it big."

"I'd love to see your work."

The echo of Claire's request was disconcerting. Riley started to invite Morgan to the gallery opening, but she stopped. The invite seemed too intimate for someone associated with her father.

Morgan seemed to sense her discomfort and pushed past the unanswered request. She pointed at the card in Riley's hand. "Call me anytime. Seriously, I've really enjoyed working on your dad's case and I'm happy to answer any questions you have that might come up later. Let me know if you change your mind about attending the hearing. I'm meeting with your mom and dad before it starts, and I know a semi-secret way to get past the press. You're welcome to join us."

Riley nodded, but she had no intention of taking her up on the offer. As she walked back to her car, she reflected on the meeting. She wasn't sure what she'd expected when she'd set up the meeting with her father's attorney, but a smart, savvy, sharp woman like Morgan Bradley hadn't been it. Everything about Morgan, including her passion for her point of view, reminded Riley of a slightly older version of Claire. Morgan's advice about not talking to Claire again replayed in her mind. It was good advice and she resolved to follow it, because talking to Claire always left her with a jumbled mix of feelings, part annoyed, but mostly intrigued.

Chapter Thirteen

Claire glanced over at Nick who was staring straight ahead, his hands gripping the steering wheel. It was Wednesday evening, and they were on their way to Buster Creel's house. They'd been stuck in traffic for thirty minutes with little but the music from the radio to fill the tense air between them. They hadn't exchanged more than a few words in the last two days, and Claire missed their playful banter. It was quickly becoming clear that it would be up to her to break the ice.

She reached into her bag. "I found these new energy bars. They're made of pretzels, sriracha, honey, and peanuts. Sweet and savory, the perfect combo." She set one on the console. "Thank me later."

"I'm good."

"Seriously, Nick, are you going to stay mad at me forever?"

"I'm not mad at you."

"Annoyed then."

"Maybe a little." He looked over at her. "Can you blame me?"

She couldn't. If he'd been sneaking around, talking to witnesses and ordering surveillance on suspects without checking with her first, she would've given him an ultimatum—work with her or find a new partner. Whatever she tried to tell herself, her encounters with Riley Flynn should be out front and open, and hiding them meant the feelings she was concerned might take over already had. If she were in a twelve-step program, it would be time for the one about admitting the exact nature of her wrongs. And it must be wrong, or she wouldn't be trying to hide it, right?

There was only one way to make sure she didn't do any permanent damage to her relationship with Nick. "Since you're already annoyed, I may as well tell you everything." Claire took a deep breath. "I've been talking to Riley Flynn. Without you. I was with her the night before Wendy Hyatt's body was found."

Nick didn't react except to tighten his grip on the steering wheel. Claire watched him carefully as he slowed the car and pulled over into the parking lot of a convenience store on the corner of the intersection. Once the car stopped, he shifted into park and turned to face her directly.

"What did you say?"

There was no going back into hiding now. Claire plunged ahead. "I ran into Riley when I was headed into Jill Shasta's funeral. She was on her way to teach a class and I caught up with her after, hoping she might be more willing to talk one-on-one. We went to Mia's and ate dinner and I asked her about the case. She didn't tell me jack shit."

"I don't even know what to say to you right now."

"Well, say something because I can tell you're mad."

"You're the one who's mad, like mad crazy. What time did you finish dinner? Where did she go afterward? You know that Reyes said the time of death could be as early as Thursday evening, right? Riley could've left you, killed Hyatt, and dumped her at the bridge that night. And you're worried about *me* being mad?"

Claire wanted to argue with him, tell him the Riley she'd spent time with was unlikely to be the killer, but he was right that she'd been careless, and she was tired of being out of sorts with her partner. "I should've told you."

"You think?" Nick's voice was raised, a rare occurrence. "Okay, maybe I was mad. You should've told me, but more than that, what were you thinking having dinner with her?"

She hadn't been thinking, but there was no sense pointing out the obvious. She didn't have anything to say other than it felt right at the time, which was the real issue distilled down to its finest point. Her attraction to Riley felt right no matter how much she knew it wasn't. She didn't expect anyone else to understand, not even Nick who knew her better than most. She settled on a partial truth. "I thought if I met with her one-on-one, in a casual setting, she might open up."

"Did she?"

"Not really. I don't get the impression she's close to her father, which makes sense since he's been away for fifteen years, but she's also oddly protective of his reputation."

"Family ties are strong."

"I guess. She seems pretty conflicted about him overall."

"Did it occur to you that might be a cover?"

"Since when are you convinced she might be involved in these killings?" Claire asked. "You gave me shit for considering her in the first place."

"Yep. I dismissed your theory and that was wrong, but no more wrong than you having your own private eye party without telling me. How about we agree to work together and share information like partners are supposed to?"

Claire relaxed, relieved at the overture. "Deal. And I am sorry."

"Noted." He pulled back out onto the road. "Now that I know about the surveillance, tell me what you've found out."

"I wish I had something to report." Claire pulled up the email she'd received this morning. "Yesterday, Riley left her house around two and returned around six. She had a class downtown in the afternoon, which is likely where she was. The patrol unit didn't spot Frank leaving the house at all, but apparently he doesn't have a car, so he's a little harder to keep tabs on." She thumbed through the message. "No signs of movement at either house today."

"Well, that's not helpful, but it makes sense since Riley works at home and Frank isn't working at all." Nick pointed at the intersection ahead. "Do I take a right or left up here?"

Claire consulted the map app on her phone. "Left. Look, I know the lookout might be a waste of resources, but if it eliminates them as suspects it will tell us more than we know right now."

"Good point. We need some kind of a break."

"Speaking of which, I'm still set on going to the Lofton Gallery tomorrow. If we can't pinpoint Riley as the artist of the sketches we have after that, then it's time to start showing these sketches far and wide."

"We could start by showing them to Buster today. He's bound to know if the artist is someone in the group."

Claire considered the idea. "We could, but he might be inclined to protect whoever it is. He and Riley seem like they're friends."

"We'd at least have the opportunity to gauge his reaction in person."

"Good point. I'm conflicted. Let's play it by ear."

"Agreed. I'll follow your lead." Nick pulled over to the right in front of a line of sleek and modern condos. "We're here." He stared at the building for a moment. "You know, this isn't where I would've pictured Buster living. He struck me as more cabin in the woods than hip and trendy."

"Look at you, judging a book by its cover," Claire said. "Let's talk about how to play this."

"We need some hairs from the dog. You think of some reason why we're here and I'll pet the puppy."

"Why do you get the fun job?"

"Because you outrank me, so you get to do the hard stuff," Nick said. "There's a price for being the smart one."

"Whatever." She knew he was kidding, but it wasn't the first time lately he'd referred to her rank and the implication she wouldn't be sticking around at detective level for long. He didn't sound jealous. His tone was more wistful, like he'd miss her. If she got this promotion, she'd miss him too, and everything else about being on the ground, investigating cases.

Buster answered the door within seconds of them ringing the doorbell, a lively Boston terrier nipping at his heels. He reached down and scooped the puppy into his arms. "Sorry about that. Darcy here is incredibly friendly and as hyper as they come. I've been working on getting her not to go insane when the doorbell rings, but I have better luck simply staking out the front door when I know someone is on their way over." He motioned for them to follow him into a small living room with a southwestern decor. "Have a seat." He set Darcy down and she immediately ran to Claire who dutifully rubbed her head.

"She's adorable."

"She is. A bit rambunctious for an artist who works from home. I can't leave any of my projects out for fear she'll run headlong into an easel and send everything flying. The energy is good though. She definitely keeps me on alert."

"I can only imagine."

"Can I get either of you something to drink?" Buster asked.

"We're good, thanks," Nick said. "We just have a few follow-up questions."

"Let me guess, that body that was found last Friday has something to do with the one you found in Deep Ellum?"

Claire risked a quick look at Nick who looked as surprised as she was by the question. She raised her eyebrows and cut her eyes to Buster, telegraphing to Nick to tread carefully.

"We can't comment on an open investigation, but we are exploring all possible angles. Do you know Wendy Hyatt?"

"Never heard of her until her name was in the paper, but the basic description stood out. Twenty-something white female," Buster said. "Sad news for sure. Both women were so young."

"They were."

"If there's a serial killer on the loose, you really should tell people. It seems like the responsible thing to do."

Would a killer offer that kind of advice? Claire considered and decided he might if he was trying to throw them off his trail. She took a moment to assess Buster as a potential killer. He was a nice-looking guy, although a little scruffy. If he'd approached Jill or Wendy, they likely wouldn't have been on alert for danger. He looked more like someone's nice uncle than a strangler. He was medium height, thin, but wiry. She'd read on his website that he built his own frames and woodworking was one of his hobbies, and she extrapolated from that he had enough muscle to strangle a victim, especially one who had been dosed with GHB.

Claire glanced at Nick. She knew she was supposed to cover for him so he could get hairs from the pup, but she decided to take a risk on an idea of her own. "I hate to ask this, but do you mind if I use your restroom?"

Buster smiled. "No problem at all. There's one down that hall to the right of the guest room."

Claire ignored Nick's questioning look and walked down the hall. When she was completely out of sight, she pressed on the door farthest from the living room, pleased when it opened into what appeared to be the master suite. She listened closely to Nick's and Buster's voices, distant now, and decided to risk a moment of snooping around.

His incredibly tidy room made her feel like a slob in contrast. She was usually very tidy as well, but she'd been off-kilter the past two weeks and the result was piles of laundry and an unmade bed. She walked past his king-sized bed and glanced into the open doors of his closet. His wardrobe was casual overall with a couple of suits hanging toward the back. She kept going, crossing the threshold to the master bath. A quick sweep of the crystal clean room revealed a bottle of generic ibuprofen and an economy-sized bottle of contact lens solution.

She hadn't really expected to find a partially used bottle of GHB sitting on the bathroom counter, but she'd held out hope she'd find some kind of clue pointing away from Riley. She took one last look around and tiptoed back to the bedroom door when she heard the muffled snorts of Buster's Boston terrier followed by Nick's raised voice.

"Hey, Darcy, come play with me."

"Don't mind her," Buster said. "Once she gets obsessed with something, she's tenacious as hell."

Claire could hear footfalls on the wood floors, headed her way, and then Nick's voice again followed by the scamper of dog feet, away from her this time. "Come here, Darcy. Good girl, Darcy. Good girl."

"She likes you," Buster said. "She almost never comes to someone that quickly."

"Dogs love me," Nick said.

Claire rolled her eyes and eased the bedroom door back into the almost closed position she'd found it in. She walked across the hall, opened the guest bathroom door, and flushed the toilet and then ran the faucet. A moment later, she slipped out of the bathroom, loudly closed the door, and walked back into the living room. She grinned at Nick. "Did I hear you getting attached to this nice doggie?" She bent down to pet Darcy's head. "She's a cutie for sure."

"Oh, I'm very attached," Nick said, giving her a wink. "A second ago, Buster looked the other way and I was considering ducking out of here with this sweet little girl."

Claire took his words as a sign he'd managed to get some of the dog's hair while she was in Buster's bedroom. All she wanted to do now was get out of there as fast as they could, but they hadn't really asked him anything and she didn't want to raise suspicions. "One of the other members of your sketch group said that you all met up at the bridge last month. I'm sure it's nothing, but it is kind of a strange coincidence that we've found two dead bodies in locations that seem to be popular spots. Do you recall seeing anything or anyone out of the ordinary at any of your meet-ups?"

Buster rubbed his chin. "I can't think of anything offhand. We usually get a fair number of people stopping to see what we're doing. People like watching us draw and sometimes they're even aspiring artists who're interested in joining the club. Just in the last six months, we've had a couple of people join that way. Warren and Jensen for example."

Claire consulted the list of artists in the group. They hadn't spoken with either of these people and she immediately moved their names up in importance. She wasn't sure why—maybe it was simply the desire to divert attention from Riley, but she needed the focus to point elsewhere. "Are they amateur artists or pros like you?"

Buster laughed. "My pro status changes from time to time. I'm doing well right now, but if we get another dip in the economy, art is one of the things people give up first, and I'll be eating ramen again. The kind from the grocery store aisle, not the fancy Japanese restaurant kind. Of all the people in our group, I'd only consider a few professional artists." He ticked names off on his fingers. "Riley Flynn has been an art instructor for a while, and she just signed on with the Lofton. Natalie Solis has sold several pieces to galleries around town. Other than that, most of the people who participate are doing it as a hobby."

Claire noted the way he smiled when he said Natalie's name, and she remembered them sitting close the first time she'd seen them at the bar. "Are you and Natalie a couple?"

"Couple? We're a bit more casual than that. We've known each other for a long time and we've dated on and off." He scrunched his forehead. "Is that important to your case?"

Claire smiled. "Not at all. I noticed your easy affection with each other the first time we talked and thought it was sweet is all." She changed the subject quickly. "Is there anything else you think might be helpful?"

"Not really." He reached for Darcy and rubbed her ears. "Have you had a chance to talk to everyone on the list I gave you?"

"Almost," Claire said. "We appreciate your help." She stood, ready to get out of there and get the dog hairs to Reyes. "Thanks again."

She and Nick were almost to the door, when Buster called out for them to wait. He reached for a pad of paper and scrawled a note and handed it to her. "Our next meet-up is Saturday. Feel free to stop by. You might be able to catch the people you haven't talked to yet."

She glanced at the note. *Farmer's Market 2 p.m.* "Thanks. We might drop by."

She and Nick had just gotten in the car when both of their phones started buzzing. She read the text on hers, while Nick answered his call. *RF hasn't left the house all day. Just had food delivered. Probably in for the night.* She started to type a reply, but Nick's voice interrupted her thoughts.

"We have another one."

"What?"

"That was dispatch. There's another body. South side of Old Red," he said, referring to the original red sandstone Dallas courthouse that was now a museum. "White, twenties, female, strangled. Ready to roll?"

Claire stared at the screen on her phone, anxious to send some texts of her own. "Feel like driving?"

Nick was out of the car in a flash and they switched places. As he sped downtown, she checked in with the unit outside Frank Flynn's place. *Status?*

Left about four hours ago. Hasn't been back.

Stay close. Text me when he shows up.

She switched back to the other text. *DO NOT lose sight of her. No matter what. If she leaves, follow and text me location.*

Claire hit send and set the phone down. Nick looked over at her. "Any news?"

"No."

"Maybe it's not the same MO," he said. "Could be a copycat."

"I guess we'll know in a few minutes." Claire wanted to say more, but all she could think about was how relieved she was that Riley was at home and had been all day. But what if they found another sketch and it turned out to be Riley's? What would that mean for the case? And what would it mean for Riley?

Chapter Fourteen

Riley lowered the blinds and dimmed the lights. Her studio had been flooded with light all day, and she blinked to adjust to the sudden change. Today had been a good day. She'd rolled out of bed, brewed a pot of tea, and spent hours painting. No weights to lift, no classes to teach, no parents or detectives dropping by to pull her into drama and intrigue that wasn't hers.

Of course, not every interaction with Claire had been unpleasant. She'd actually enjoyed both of the meals they'd shared at Mia's, and even though she'd stalked out of the last one, she could admit at least fifty percent of that had been about her own sensitivity about her father. He was a complicated issue, and she didn't expect anyone to understand how she could love the memory of the man she'd known and feel sorry for what he'd gone through, but still hold on to residual anger about the big gaps in her life because he lacked good character.

Lacked. The mistakes he made were fifteen years in the past. What if he really was a changed person, more like the man from her childhood than the one who'd ripped it away? If he was, how would that manifest now? It was too late for things like teaching her to drive, giving advice about college, or any of the other father-daughter things a teenage girl should be able to expect from her dad. Could he possibly have some role in her life now that wasn't tangled up in anything to do with his court case? She rubbed her forehead with the heel of her hand, unable to process the possibilities and the risk of wanting what might only be a mirage. Maybe someday.

Riley walked through her studio, picking up stray brushes and tubes of paint to be cleaned and stored. While she was painting, she was a tornado, more concerned about plowing forward than leaving a tidy trail in her wake. When the room resembled a living space instead of an artist studio, she poured an inch of Jameson's and sank onto the couch.

Thoughts of her father led her to think about Claire, and Riley wondered if she were similarly tucked away in her own home with the spirit of her choice. Did Claire share her love of a well-lit apartment or would she be more of a house with a yard kind of person? Was she neat and orderly or too busy to care about mundane things like household order? Riley sipped her whiskey and let her mind wander and body relax. For the first time in days, contentment was not a stranger and she slipped into an easy slumber.

Bang, bang, bang.

Riley shot awake and rushed to focus on her surroundings. Whiskey glass mostly full. Surrounded by couch cushions. Lights dimmed. Slowly, she reached the conclusion she'd dozed off and now someone was at her door, rapid-fire knocking to get her attention. Three more knocks in quick succession made it clear they were not going away. "I'm coming. I'm coming," she said.

She reached the door and peered out the viewer to see Claire with her hand raised, looking harried. For a second, Riley wondered if she was dreaming since she'd been thinking about Claire as she'd fallen asleep.

"Riley, let me in."

Nope, not dreaming. She turned the locks and opened the door partway, cautious, but curious about whatever it was that seemed so urgent. "What's going on?" she asked. "What time is it?"

"It's late. Can I come in?"

Riley didn't have to think about it. She wanted to know what was going on, but even more, she felt oddly glad Claire was here—a sensation she filed away to process later. "Yes." She swung the door open wide, closing and locking it again after Claire walked through. She motioned to the couch. "Have a seat. Would you like some tea?"

"Coffee?"

"Sorry, tea is all I have, but if you're looking for caffeine, I have a great British blend that's even better than coffee for a boost."

Claire bit her bottom lip which Riley recognized as her I'm thinking about it look. It was endearing, and Riley wondered when she'd made the shift from finding Claire abrasive to feeling affection for her.

"I'll take some tea. Although I must say it's a travesty that you don't have coffee."

"Noted." Riley walked over to the kitchen and filled the electric kettle and set it to boil. She set up another cup with a bag of her favorite blend and turned back to Claire. "I have a feeling you didn't drop by just to get a hot drink."

"No." Claire ran a hand through her hair, clearly stressed. "Another body turned up tonight."

Riley sagged against the kitchen counter. "Oh no. That's horrible." She studied Claire's distraught expression. "Are you okay?"

"What?" Claire shook her head. "Yes. I mean, no, not really."

"Was she…like the others?" Riley hoped Claire would know what she was asking without making her say the words.

"Early twenties. We have a tentative ID based on a report filed by her roommate with campus security at Richards. If we're right, she was a first year law student."

"What a waste." Riley started to reach for Claire's hand to offer reassurance, but she stopped midway, unsure how the gesture would be received. "I can tell you're taking this hard."

"Three murders in less than three weeks. Not a great track record."

Riley responded to the despair in Claire's voice. "It's not like you're responsible."

"It's my job to stop this from happening."

The kettle whistled to signal the water was ready, and Riley poured it into Claire's cup. She brought it to Claire. "Let this steep for a bit. Cream or sugar?"

"This is good. Thanks."

Claire fiddled with the tag on the tea bag, and Riley's heart melted a little at her obvious vulnerability. "I'm happy to be a beverage stop for your evening, but is there some other reason you came by?"

"Yes," Claire said. She set the tea cup down, reached into her bag, and pulled out her phone. "I need to show you something."

Riley watched with a sense of dread and excitement as Claire tapped on her phone. A moment later, Claire thrust the phone toward her. It took Riley a moment to focus on the three-way split screen. She reached for the phone and used her thumb and forefinger to enlarge the familiar images, sucking in a breath when she recognized what she was seeing. "Where did you get these?"

"Are they yours?"

Riley stared at the images. The mural in Deep Ellum, the Margaret Hunt Hill Bridge, the Old Red Courthouse. Rough sketches, the beginnings of work that would be featured in her upcoming show. These were the drawings she'd been looking for, the ones Lacy had requested, in the sketchbook she couldn't find. How had they wound up on Claire's phone? She asked again. "Where did you get these?"

Claire reached for the phone and looked at the screen as she spoke. "One from each murder scene. Tucked away in the pockets of the murdered women, like little tokens the killer wanted us to find." Claire looked back up at her. "I answered you, now it's your turn. Are they yours?"

Riley sank onto the couch. "Yes." Her brain started churning, trying to process exactly what it meant that her sketches had shown up at murder scenes. Had she just made tea for the woman who was about to arrest her? She wanted to make a strong declaration, but instead she barely managed a whispered response. "I didn't kill those women."

"I know."

"How?"

"We've had a squad car watching your house. You didn't leave all day. Whoever killed the woman we found tonight did it a few hours ago, and I don't have any doubt it's the same person that killed the others."

Riley set aside her anger about being watched for a second and focused on the big picture. "Then why are you here?"

"Because I had to know if you were the artist behind the sketches. Don't you see? These killings are tied to you somehow."

"Wait." Riley struggled to follow, fighting sleepy brain and an already confusing mix of detail. "I thought you said you know I didn't do it."

"No, but someone did, and I'm thinking you have a clue even if you don't know what it is. Did you give these sketches to someone?"

What Claire said made sense, but Riley didn't have any ideas that might help. "I didn't, but I did have a sketchbook go missing. I was looking for it last week. The gallery wanted some of my early sketches. I thought I'd misplaced the sketchbook, but it looks like whoever did this, has it."

Claire nodded. "Try to remember the last time you had it. Was it here or maybe you left it somewhere when you were out drawing with the group?"

Riley tried to focus, but her mind was a jumbled mix of thoughts and feelings, not leaving much room for memories to surface. "I don't remember." A flash of a recollection surfaced. "No, wait. I did have it with me when we were at Old Red a month or so ago. Wait. Let me see your phone again."

Claire handed it over and Riley stared at the images, drawings she'd sketched under a sunny Dallas sky, surrounded by friends. She flicked through the photos, stopping at the one of her drawing of Old Red, and a sick knot twisted her insides. She pointed at the screen. "This is the last sketch I drew in that sketchbook. I remember filling the pages and switching to another book that day. I stowed this one in my bag, but I don't have any recollection of what I did with it after that. I went looking for it when I signed on with the Lofton Gallery, but I couldn't find it anywhere."

"When were you at Old Red? Who else was there?"

"I can get the exact date. And I'm sure Buster has a list of who was there. He keeps track of that kind of stuff. Do you think someone else in the group took my notebook? But wouldn't that mean…"

Claire shook her head. "We're getting ahead of ourselves. I'm just trying to cover all the bases. I'll talk to Buster. It would be best if you didn't tell anyone what I've told you."

"Am I one of the bases?" Riley asked. "Or have you finally come to the conclusion I'm not a criminal?"

"I'm not going to lie. You've been a person of interest. Can you blame me? You were at or nearby the first two murder scenes. The victims had sketches on them. And…"

Riley waited a moment, but Claire didn't finish her sentence, so she finished it for her. "And my father is a convicted murderer."

"I'd be lying if I said his past didn't factor into the equation." Claire looked pained. "We've had a car parked at his place as well as yours."

"And?"

"Have you talked to him today?"

Riley heard Morgan Bradley's voice in her head, telling her not to talk to Claire, that all she cared about was making her case. She didn't have anything to hide, but did Frank? She settled on asking a question of her own. "Why?"

Claire grimaced like she was trying to decide if she should answer, but Riley waited her out. Finally, Claire said, "He hasn't been home for hours. If you know where he is you could provide him with an alibi."

"Why would my father kill these women, and even if he did, why would he leave my drawings at the scene of a crime? It doesn't make sense." She watched Claire's face for her reaction and was rewarded with a nod.

"You're right. It doesn't make sense." Claire picked up her teacup and took a deep drink. "None of this makes sense, but the more clues I can eliminate the better equipped I'll be to find the truth. Part of my job is asking hard questions, but I get how invasive and annoying it can be. Hell, I was about to storm the Lofton when they reopen tomorrow and demand to see your work so I could tell if it matched the sketches we found."

Riley took a moment to consider Claire's words. She sounded perfectly reasonable, and her expression and tone were earnest and respectful. It was Claire's job to find the truth, and Riley's gut told her that was all Claire was trying to do. Maybe it was time to set aside her naturally suspicious thoughts and give Claire the benefit of the doubt. "I don't know anything about where my father was today or pretty much any day. But when it comes to my work, there's no need to storm the gallery. I would've shown it to you if you'd told me why you needed to see it."

Claire's face softened into a smile. "I know that's right. I apologize for not being direct with you. I really would like to see your work, and not just because of this case."

"Well, I'll be at the gallery tomorrow going over some plans for the installation. Care to join me?"

"I'd love to," Claire said without a moment's hesitation. "Full disclosure, I'll be looking for clues. There's clearly some connection between your sketches and the killer's choice of locations to dump the bodies."

"The murders are taking place somewhere else then?" Riley asked. She wasn't sure why it mattered to her, but now that she was close to this case, she wanted to know every detail.

"It's not entirely clear yet. But back to your sketches. I don't suppose you remember what else was in the missing sketchbook."

"I don't." In response to Claire's look of disappointment, Riley added, "But I could review our meet-up schedule for the past few months and get pretty close. I'll bring a list when I meet you at the gallery tomorrow."

"That would be great." Claire stood. "What time should I meet you there?"

Riley cursed her clumsy wording that had apparently given Claire the impression it was time for her to go. Setting aside the reason for Claire's visit, she'd enjoyed Claire's company and wished they were two people having tea, discussing their days without a murder in the mix. She wanted to extend an invitation to stay, but Claire was working and no matter how much she'd allowed herself to lapse into a feeling of comfort, this visit had been professional, not personal. "The gallery opens at noon. Let's meet then."

"That sounds perfect." Claire met her eyes, and for a moment they were locked in a visual embrace, trepidatious and tender, neither seeming to want to let go. Riley held her breath, wondering what it meant and allowing hope to enter in.

CHAPTER FIFTEEN

Claire rolled over in bed and slapped the nightstand until she found her buzzing phone. Through barely open eyelids, she read the screen. Seven a.m. She supposed she should be grateful for the three hours of sleep she'd had, but it was too damn early to think of anything but coffee. She sat up in bed and opened the text that had roused her from her slumber. It was from Nick, who'd apparently been busy since she'd left him at the scene the night before.

Campus cops confirmed vic ID. Leah Tosca. Parents out of country. Have a call in to roommate. Interviews lined up with Warren and Jensen this morning. Want me to drive?

She typed back. *Nice try. I'll pick you up at 8:30.*

Next up, coffee. Claire ground the beans and measured enough scoops for her to be able to take an extra mug for Nick. The act reminded her of Riley making tea for them the night before, and she allowed herself a few moments of reflection. She'd shown up at Riley's last night under the guise of performing her duty as a cop, but she could've asked Riley to come to the station to meet with her and Nick to look at the sketches, instead of showing up, late at night and unannounced. To her credit, she hadn't lied to Nick about where she was going, but she had pulled rank and told him to stay at the scene and oversee the collection of evidence while she acted on impulses that were entirely unrelated to duty and fully focused on the opportunity to see Riley under better circumstances than the way they'd parted at Mia's the last time they'd met.

On a personal level, she had no regrets. Riley had been more relaxed and open, and Claire hadn't wanted to leave the easy comfort they'd managed to find after all their initial encounters had been full of agitation and acrimony. For a few moments, the ugliness that had brought them together faded away, and Claire imagined what life would be like if she had an intelligent and creative woman like Riley to come home to at the end of the day.

The coffee maker dinged, and she dismissed her dreamy thoughts. Riley wasn't her girlfriend. Up until yesterday, she'd been a person of interest in a murder case, and but for these murders, they might have never met. The truth was harsh, and Claire wished it were different, but she had to keep her focus on this case and set aside anything that might distract her from her job.

An hour later, she pulled up to the curb outside of Nick's house. She texted him to say she was waiting outside and took advantage of the wait to check her growing email inbox. When she heard a rap on the window, she looked up to see Nick's wife, Cheryl, standing beside her car, and she motioned for her to open the door.

"Hi, Claire," Cheryl said. "Nick had a wardrobe malfunction—he told me not to tell you that—but he'll be right out."

"Let me guess, he wound up wearing his breakfast."

"Yes, but if you tell him I told you, I'll deny it with my last breath." Cheryl pointed into the car and, at Claire's nod, slid into the passenger's seat. "Actually, I came out because I wanted to invite you to dinner tonight. You two have been working round the clock and so have I. We all deserve to relax and share a good meal and a bottle of wine, don't you think?"

The offer was tempting. Claire had been their guest several times before and the three of them always had a good time, sharing food and stories about their work in a mutual effort to burn off steam from their high stress jobs. "I'd love to, really, but this case is blowing up. We've got a full day, and I have a feeling we're headed for double overtime."

"Fine, we'll skip the wine, but you've got to eat. If you want to, you can bounce ideas off me, but I haven't seen Nick in a while, and if you're working, he's working. So, work here tonight, and do us both a favor."

"I can't argue with that logic," Claire said.

"What logic is that?" Nick asked, appearing at the car window. "Claire, are you trying to steal my wife?"

"Caught me." She held up her hands, wrists together. "Seriously, you better get in the car before I race off with her."

Cheryl laughed and traded places with Nick, but before Claire could drive away, she said, "I'm holding you to your promise."

"What was that all about?" Nick asked as Claire pulled away from the curb.

"Your wife just ordered us to a working dinner at your place tonight. There might be wine. Damn, I hope there's wine."

Nick sighed. "Resisting Cheryl is futile when she has her mind set on something." He gave her the address for their first stop. "You learn anything else from Flynn last night?"

His referring to Riley by her last name only was jarring, like she was still a suspect instead of someone who might be able to assist their investigation. She'd texted Nick when she'd left Riley's to let him know that Riley had confirmed the sketches were hers, but she hadn't told him anything else about their conversation. Reviewing it in her head now, she realized there wasn't much to tell. Telling Nick about her growing attraction for Riley was a no-go, and it didn't have anything to do with the case. She did a mental run-through of everything they'd discussed. "I asked her about her father, who showed up at his place around midnight, by the way. She hasn't had much contact with him since he was released."

"And you believe her?"

His question didn't have any tone, but it put Claire on the defensive, nonetheless. "I do. Besides, it doesn't make sense that her father would kill these women and slip a sketch his daughter drew into their pockets," she said, echoing Riley's statement from last night. "What would be the point?"

"I don't know," Nick said. "But I'm not sure there's a point to any of these killings."

"There is, but we're going to have to dig deeper to find it. Any news from Reyes about the dog hairs you snagged from Buster's dog?"

"Darcy has been exonerated. The hairs don't match. Buster did send over the list of all the locations for the Eastside Sketchers for the past six months along with which members were at each meet-up. Warren and Jensen were at all of them, along with Buster and Natalie. The other members were hit and miss."

"Okay." Claire wasn't sure what conclusions to draw and decided to mull over the information for now, since they had arrived at Warren Spencer's house in east Dallas, a modest ranch-style brick house with several large trees in the front yard. The trees reminded her of her promise to get a yard service over to her parents' house, and she took a moment to send a quick text to a yard service while Nick reviewed his notes. "Tell me what you know about Mr. Spencer."

"Not much. He's a retired commercial architect. Does some consulting on the side. Buster said he happened upon their group one day and thought it would be cool to draw something other than building plans. He's been joining their meet-ups for a few months."

Claire made a mental note to ask Riley her own impression of Warren when she saw her later, and she realized the anticipation of seeing her again had her a bit distracted. "Why don't you take the lead on this one," she said.

"You got it."

They walked to the door and Nick rang the bell. A couple of minutes later, a handsome older man answered the door. "Mr. Spencer?" At his nod, Nick introduced himself and Claire. "May we come in?"

"Of course, but please call me Warren." Warren stepped back and ushered them in and led them into the living area. "Have a seat. Can I get you anything?"

"We're good," Nick said. "We just have a few questions."

"About those girls, right. Buster said you've been talking to everyone."

Claire ground her teeth at the word "girls," but decided if she could forgive her father for the oversight, she could forgive this guy who looked to be about the same age. She listened while Nick went through the litany of questions they'd asked the other members of the Eastside Sketchers, growing bored when they got the same answers. Didn't see anything unusual, didn't notice anyone acting strangely, didn't know jack. She distracted herself by looking around the room, her gaze settling on a grouping of framed photos on the end table a few feet away.

"That's my daughter," Warren said. "On her wedding day. Sixteen years ago."

Claire experienced a twinge of embarrassment at having been caught spying—the being caught part—but she decided to go all in. She picked up the photo and stared at the wedding party. A handsome groom, a beautiful bride, flanked by Warren and another woman. Claire pointed at the photo. "Is this your wife?"

"Yes. She died earlier this year."

"I'm so sorry."

"Don't be. She had cancer and she was in a lot of pain. She's with her other loved ones now." Despite his assurances, his eyes welled up with tears.

Claire nodded, hoping they could get out of there before she stepped in any other emotional landmines. Thankfully, Nick piped up to say they should get going. When they were back out in the car, he gave her a hard time. "Way to pick on the old man and make him cry."

"I know. Couldn't feel worse." She drove to the end of the street. "That was a bust. Where are we headed next?"

Nick directed her to an address farther north, close to White Rock Lake. The apartment complex backed up to one of the parks close to the lake and provided easy access to pedestrian and cycling trails. They were on their way to the building when a cyclist rode up to them, stopped, and removed his helmet.

"Let me guess, you're the detectives." the cyclist said, running a hand through his thick, wavy dark hair.

Claire couldn't help but return his infectious smile, and she stuck out her hand. "And here we thought we were the detectives. I'm Claire Hanlon and this is my partner, Nick Redding. And you must be Jensen Pierce."

"I am." He shook her hand and Nick's. "Sorry, I'm late. I decided to get in a quick ride but blew a tire halfway through and had to borrow a tube to get back on the road." He lifted his bike with one hand and pointed to the building with the other. "Let's go inside."

She and Nick followed him into a small studio apartment. Jensen placed his bike on the wall mount and hung his helmet on the handlebars.

"I'm having a protein shake. Can I get either of you anything?"

"We're good," Claire said. "We won't keep you long. We just have a few questions."

Jensen grimaced. "Buster said you'd be calling. Are you close to catching the crazy stalker who's killing these women? Rumor has it the latest one goes to Richards."

"Did you know her?"

"No. I think she was in law school and I'm merely an up-and-coming artist, but if you check out all the posts, everyone loved her. Of course, most of the people saying that probably didn't even know her. Social media brings out the fakers." He pulled a bottle from the fridge and joined them in the main living area. "What other questions do you have?"

Claire asked him the standard set of questions they'd asked everyone else, but like everyone else, Jensen had nothing to report as far as any unusual activity during any of their outings, including the last one in Deep Ellum. "Riley stuck around after the rest of us left. She'd be the most likely person to have seen anything out of the ordinary. She's an incredible artist and has a fantastic eye for detail."

Despite the hyperbole, Claire sensed his praise was genuine and she felt oddly proud on Riley's behalf. "Have you known her long?"

"Since I joined the group last year. I tried to get into one of her classes this semester, but they fill up fast."

Claire exchanged a glance with Nick, wishing he could read her mind so they could confer about what she wanted to ask next, but he couldn't so she decided to toss it out there and see what happened. "Have you ever borrowed any of Riley's sketchbooks? Like to learn technique?" She watched for Jensen's reaction, ready to pounce at the first sign of guilt. All she got was a puzzled look.

"No, but she probably would've loaned it to me if I'd asked. She's very generous with her time and talent. She even lets me tag along sometimes when she goes out to sketch on her own. She and Buster are the best artists in the group."

That was it. Claire was convinced Jensen was an authentic member of the Riley Flynn fan club. "Good to know. Is there anything else we should know?"

"No, but I'll let you know if I think of anything." He raised his protein drink in salute. "I hope you catch this guy soon."

"We do too," Claire said. She handed Jensen a card and then led the way for her and Nick to leave. Once they were back in the car, Nick said, "Well, looks like you have competition for your Riley love-fest."

"What the hell is that supposed to mean?"

"Whoa, don't get mad. I was kidding. Let's not fight again. I can't handle working these long hours if my snack buddy isn't going to speak to me."

"Maybe not so much with the picking on the snack buddy for you," she said with a forced smile.

"How about we grab an early lunch? My treat."

"As much as I'd like to let you buy me a meal, I'm meeting Riley at the gallery at noon. I thought it would be good to go through her work and see if it triggers anything about the case and get an idea of what other local landmarks might be on the killer's list." She paused, and then added. "You're welcome to come if you want."

Nick met her eyes and shook his head. "No, you've developed a rapport with her. You don't need someone else in there messing it up. You go and I'll see if we can get something scheduled with Tosca's roommate."

"Sounds good." Claire hoped her relief wasn't too visible. At this point, she was still pretending her interest in Riley was purely professional, but she wasn't ready for anyone else to know the truth.

Chapter Sixteen

Riley stood in the center of the gallery doing her best to pay attention to Lacy while keeping her eye on the door. Claire had said she'd be here at noon, but it was half past, and Riley was convinced she wasn't coming.

"And I think this piece would look best over here."

Riley tore her attention from Claire-watch back to Lacy. "I'm sorry, what?"

"Are you okay? You seem distracted today." Lacy put a hand on her arm as she asked the question, her eyes reflecting sincere concern.

"Sorry. I had trouble sleeping last night," Riley said, leaving out the part about how dreams of Claire and subsequent hours of wondering what the dreams meant had kept her up through the night. She smiled to reassure Lacy. "I promise you have my full attention."

At that moment, the gallery door swung open and both of them turned at the sound. Claire was framed in the doorway, more beautiful than any of the artwork hanging on the walls inside, and Riley could not stop staring, surprised at how much she'd been looking forward to seeing her. She spent a split second trying to regain her self-control before abandoning the effort in favor of a smile and a step in Claire's direction, barely noticing when Lacy's hand dropped from her arm. "You made it."

Claire's warm smile reached into her eyes. "Sorry, I'm late. My appointment ran long. Is it still okay that I came?"

"Of course." Riley looked back at Lacy, feeling the heat of a blush when she caught Lacy's knowing glance at Claire. "Detective Claire Hanlon, this is Lacy Lofton, the gallery owner. We were going over the details of the installation."

"Nice to meet you, Detective," Lacy said, extending her hand.

"Just Claire is fine, thanks." Claire clasped Lacy's hand, but her eyes were on Riley who stood to the side, processing exactly how happy she was to see Claire and what that meant.

"Are you here in some official capacity?" Lacy asked.

"Claire wanted to see my work, and I asked her to stop by," Riley said, hoping it was okay with Claire that she glossed over the real reason for her visit. "You don't mind, do you?"

"Of course not. It's your work, after all," Lacy said. "I have a couple of calls to make. Why don't the two of you look around and I'll be back in a few." She waved at Claire as she walked away. "Nice to meet you, Detective."

Once she was out of sight, Claire said, "I'm sorry. Pretty clear I interrupted you."

"No, it's fine."

"Are you sure?" Claire dropped her voice to a whisper. "I think the gallery owner is smitten with her new artist."

Riley felt the burn of a blush again, hotter this time, as her mind clicked through the few small instances over the past couple of weeks when she'd wondered if Lacy was flirting with her. If there were feelings, she didn't reciprocate, and it was ironic that the person pointing out Lacy's flirting was the one person she was attracted to, and that only intensified the heat. She let it simmer for a moment until a new feeling boiled to the surface. "Are you implying the gallery is representing me because she likes me, not my art?"

"What?" Claire's expression turned to shock instantly. "No. Absolutely not." She pointed to her painting of the Eye, propped up against the counter. "I mean look at this. You're an amazing artist. Any gallery would be lucky to have you."

Riley wanted to believe her, and for a moment she allowed herself to embrace the compliment and bask in the glow of its warmth. Was this how it felt to be appreciated for who she was, not viewed through the lens of her father's transgressions? She craved more, but was leery it wouldn't last, so she shifted into work mode. "You wanted to look at my other drawings for your case?"

Claire's slightly raised eyebrow signaled she noticed the change from friendly to professional, but she didn't remark on it. "Yes. I'm not sure how helpful it will be, but I thought if I had an idea of the places you've drawn, it might lead to some clues."

"You think he'll strike again?"

Claire bit her lower lip, and Riley knew she'd hit a chord. "It's okay. You don't have to tell me." She motioned to the right. "Come on." She led the way into the inner room. Lacy was on the phone in the back of the room and she waved, rolling her hand in the air to signal whoever was on the other end of the call was droning on. Riley waved back, secretly glad to have this time alone with Claire. She reached for her portfolio and spread it out on the counter. "These are my favorite spots. They'll be featured in the show." She flipped through the pages, pointing out the ones Claire was already familiar with, more refined sketches of the mural, the bridge, and the courthouse. She turned the page and pointed. "These sketches are from the arboretum. I love to watch the sailboats on White Rock Lake." She turned the page to a scene of a bustling market, featuring booths full of sculptures and paintings and artists in front of easels.

"That looks familiar."

"It's the Deep Ellum Art Festival." Riley laughed. "Very meta, and not my usual style, but I had fun. That wasn't one we did as a group. I love sketching at markets and festivals. Great people watching—the interaction between buyers and browsers and sellers."

"Aren't the Eastside Sketchers going to the Farmer's Market this weekend? Buster mentioned it."

"Yes, but I was thinking of skipping. I'm weirded out at the idea a murderer is using my drawings as inspiration."

"I hear you, but I was hoping you'd be there since I was thinking about tagging along."

"You were, huh? Considering quitting the cop gig for a career as an artist?"

Claire laughed. "Hardly. I can barely draw a stick figure. We've talked to almost everyone in your group, but I thought it might be a good idea to see how it all works in person."

It was Riley's turn to laugh. "You might be bored. We descend on a location, set up, and draw and paint for two hours. Then we go drink. There, I saved you a trip." Immediately, she wished she could reel back the words, because it would be nice to see Claire again and share her love of capturing the city's special spots in her work. And then she had another thought. "Wait a minute. Do you think someone in the group is the killer?"

"We considered that, but we've talked to everyone and it doesn't seem probable. I don't mean to creep you out, but what does seem likely is that whoever is killing these women has seen you sketching, whether with the group or when you're out on your own." Claire tapped her fingers on the counter. "Hey, do you think…"

"What?"

"Jensen said he joins you on occasion, outside of the scheduled group meetings. Would he have had a chance to snag your sketchbook on one of those outings?"

"Jensen?" Riley frowned. "Not a chance. He's a great guy. Very interested in improving his work. I let him tag along because I feel bad my classes this semester filled up before he could enroll. Besides, he's family."

"I want to think it's cute that you believe just because he's gay he couldn't also be a killer, but you must realize that's a false assumption."

"I know. I'm not that naive." Riley hunched her shoulders. "I guess I just feel like we have a bond and he wouldn't steal from me or try to set me up for murder. Make that murders." She hated the idea that people with whom she'd shared the very personal experience of creating art might violate her trust. "I guess you never really know someone."

"I don't know if that's true," Claire said, her expression thoughtful. "Getting to know someone is a process. Take us for instance. When we first met, we both had very different impressions than we do now, right?"

"True." Curiosity pressed Riley to say. "What's your impression now?"

"I have a pretty good sense of who you are. Strong, but sensitive. Creative, but practical. Guarded, but generous."

As she spoke, Claire's eyes were dark and intense and Riley didn't want to do anything to break the intimacy of the moment. If she could draw her feelings right now, the composition would be full of light and curved lines with no harsh edges to block out the connection between them.

Claire's phone buzzed, but she didn't move to reach for it. "You should get that," Riley said.

"I know," Claire said, waiting another few beats before she pulled her phone out of her pocket and looked at the screen. She sighed. "I have to go."

Riley stared at Claire's face, trying to read her expression. "It's not another…" She couldn't put her fear into words.

"No. But it is about the case." Claire reached for her hand and squeezed it. "Thank you for letting me see your work. I know how important it is to you, and I can't wait for your opening."

Riley gripped her hand and then slowly let go. "Thank you."

Claire started walking toward the door but stopped and turned back. "Do you have plans tonight?"

The question caught her off guard. "I have class until six."

"Right. It's Thursday." Claire grinned. "You would think I would remember that. I guess you're going to Mia's after."

"That's the plan. Care to join me?"

"I can't."

Riley wasn't prepared for the weight of disappointment at Claire's no. "Totally get it."

"I'm having dinner with Nick and his wife. Will you join me? At Nick's place. There won't be brisket tacos, but his wife, Cheryl, is an amazing cook. It's kind of a work thing. We were going to brainstorm about the case, so don't feel obligated to say yes. Seriously—"

"I'd love to," Riley said before Claire could babble about it anymore, though a small part of her enjoyed seeing Claire in the vulnerable role for once. "What time?"

"I'll pick you up at your place at seven."

Riley watched Claire go, more pleased than she cared to admit that she'd see her again in a few hours.

Claire stood at Riley's door, contemplating her decision about tonight. Five minutes ago, in a totally chickenshit move, she'd texted Nick to let him know she was bringing Riley, and his reply was simply *OK*. Not exactly a ringing endorsement, but if this was really a working dinner, there was no reason she shouldn't bring someone with her who might have valuable information to help them solve these murders. Riley wasn't the killer, but Claire was convinced she was the key.

She knocked and the door opened almost immediately to reveal Riley standing in front of her.

"Come in," Riley said. When Claire didn't move, she shifted from one foot to the other. "What's wrong?"

Claire smiled and shook her head. "Absolutely nothing. You look fantastic." She watched as Riley looked down at her clothes. A brown tweed blazer, crisp navy shirt, dark jeans, and burnished brown Doc Marten oxfords. She was a total smokeshow, but judging by her shy demeanor, she didn't have a clue how great she looked, which only enhanced the effect.

"I wasn't sure if tonight was casual or what. I don't have much in the way of dress up clothes, and this is about as nice as it gets."

"Nick and Cheryl are very down-to-earth. You're perfect."

Riley pointed at her. "I think you might win the perfect award. No sharp lines for you tonight?"

"Spoken like a true artist." Claire was secretly pleased Riley had noticed her outfit, which she'd stressed over. She'd abandoned her usual stuffy suits in favor of a drapey scarlet silk shirt with a slight ruffle on the cuff and her very best pair of jeans. "Are you ready?"

Riley reached over to the table by the door and grabbed a bottle of wine. "Now I am."

On the car ride over, they discussed everyday things like the weather and the Mavericks. Nothing about the case and nothing of substance, and Claire loved every word of the easy chatter. She couldn't remember the last time she'd felt so at ease with another woman, like she didn't have to be on guard, resisting the urge to talk about her job because it was either too gruesome or too time-consuming. When they finally pulled up in front of Nick's house, she'd forgotten to dread his in-person reaction at the fact she'd brought Riley along.

"Whoa," Riley said. "I thought you said these people are down-to-earth."

Claire looked at the house. She'd seen it so many times, she'd forgotten the impression the large Tudor might make on a newcomer, and she tried to see it through Riley's eyes. "Okay, it's a mansion, but in their defense, Cheryl is a highly sought-after doctor and she comes from lots of money. This was her parents' house before they relocated to Florida."

"If a butler greets us," Riley said, "I'm out of here."

Luckily, Nick answered the door. He graciously accepted the bottle of wine Riley had brought, but when her back was turned, he shook his head at Claire. She'd expected his disapproval, but she was prepared to defend her decision to bring Riley with a list of practical reasons, none of which touched on the real purpose which was simply she wanted to spend more time with her, and while this case was pending, there wouldn't be any other opportunity to do so. Plus, she had a nagging feeling Riley might be in the killer's sights, maybe not as a victim, but in some perverse way that caused her to feel protective. She didn't have it all figured out, but in the meantime, she was going to enjoy Riley's company, and Nick could get over it.

"Whatever Cheryl is cooking, it smells wonderful," she said.

"Go see for yourself," Nick said. "I've been banished for oversampling." He hefted the bottle of wine. "I'll open this and meet you in the dining room."

"Oversampling? No such thing." Claire motioned to Riley. "Come meet Cheryl. She's the one you want to get to know in this house."

They found Cheryl in the kitchen, vigorously stirring something in a pot on the stove. Claire made the introductions and noted Cheryl's glance back and forth between them like she was trying to figure out what the deal was. "Riley is helping us out with the case. She's an artist, specializing in urbanscapes. She has a show later this month at the Lofton Gallery."

"That's impressive. Lacy Lofton is a gem," Cheryl said. "She curated a display in the new cancer treatment wing of the hospital, and it's beautiful. Refused to take any payment for her services or the delivery and installation. I'm sure you'll have much success with your work at the Lofton."

"She's made me feel at home from the moment I walked in," Riley said. "And she's had a lot of great suggestions for building my portfolio. I envisioned a very different gallery experience—more formal and stuffier—and I really enjoy her hands-on style. I think it'll add to my development as an artist."

"I'd love an invite to the show if you're not already full up. I'm not the most avid collector, but I love buying art from people at the beginning of their career. Makes me feel like I'm a patron from the Renaissance. I hope you like shrimp tacos."

Claire was used to Cheryl's whiplash inducing changes of topics, but she could tell by the look on Riley's face, she was still trying to sort out if the questions were land mines or legit. "I guess I should've asked if you have any food allergies," Claire said.

"Shellfish has never done me wrong," Riley said with a grin. "And, Cheryl, I'll make sure you get an invite, but don't feel obligated to make a purchase. I'll consider it a success if anyone shows up."

Cheryl pointed a fork at Riley. "Humble." She looked at Claire. "This one's a keeper."

Claire felt the heat of the blush wash over her at Cheryl's misread of the situation between her and Riley, but there really wasn't any easy way to correct her without drawing attention to the fact there was something brewing between them no matter how much she tried to pretend their association was purely professional. Nick was right, she was blurring lines, and she should care about the implication for her career, but in this moment, all she cared about was the easy vibe of being on a double date with a catch of a date in the company of her dearest friends.

"Dinner's ready," Cheryl announced, and Nick appeared to help her carry platters into the dining room. Claire finally looked over at Riley who was grinning. Apparently, she wasn't disturbed at all to be mistaken for a couple. Claire filed that fact away and led her into the dining room.

"You have a beautiful home," Riley said as they passed the platters and started digging into the food.

"Thank you," Cheryl said. "It's way too big, but it's been in the family for years and my parents can't bear to let it go. I suggested they lease it, but not a lot of families need this much space, and it is convenient when they visit to have them be in an entirely different wing. Right, Nick?"

"I love my in-laws," he said in a perfect deadpan.

Cheryl smiled at Riley. "He practices that line when they're due for a visit. Mom and Dad are a bit hard to take. Very particular and very used to having their way. When they're here, they talk about Florida like it's paradise, and when they're there, Dallas is the only place on earth they'd rather be."

Riley laughed and Claire watched the exchange, pleased with how seamlessly Riley fit into their group.

"Do your parents live in Dallas?" Cheryl asked.

Claire looked at Nick who rolled his eyes. Clearly, he hadn't filled his wife in on Riley's background, but he'd place the fault with Claire for bringing Riley here in the first place without much in the way of notice. "Uh, Riley is—"

Riley put a hand on her arm and shook her head. She turned to Cheryl. "Yes, my parents live in Dallas, but they're divorced and we're not close. And I'm fairly certain all three of our homes would fit into this one."

Everyone laughed and Claire let out a breath, relieved and impressed Riley had handled the question with ease. She wasn't sure why she was surprised. Riley handled everything that had been thrown her way with measured steadiness, and it was one of the things she admired about her.

The rest of the dinner went without incident. When they were done and the dishes were cleared, Cheryl brought out a tray holding a clear liquor bottle and four slender stemmed glasses. She lifted the bottle. "This is Casa Dragones Joven tequila or, as I like to call it, nectar of the gods." She poured them each a glass. "I picked it up last month in Puerto Vallarta. I won't bore you with the details about how it's made. Just sip and enjoy."

Claire clinked her glass with the others and raised it to her lips, locking eyes with Riley seated across from her. For a moment, everyone else faded away and Claire imagined it was just her and Riley, enjoying each other's company, far removed from this case, these murders.

Cheryl's voice broke through her musings. "Who's ready for a game of brainstorm with the civilians? Riley, you're on my team. What's the first topic?"

Claire caught Nick looking at her out of the corner of her eye and wondered if he'd seen her staring at Riley. Wasn't much she could do about it now other than dive deep into what they'd come here for. "First topic is motive," she said. "Someone either stole or found Riley's sketchbook. Her drawings are showing up at each murder scene. The natural conclusion is someone either wants to implicate Riley in these murders or they are sending her a message."

Everyone turned to look at Riley, and Claire instantly regretted putting her on the hot seat, but she eagerly anticipated what she had to say.

"I wish I could be more helpful, but I don't have any enemies that I know of. Certainly not anyone who'd commit murder to get my attention."

Cheryl slapped her hand on the arm of her chair. "Maybe it's not about someone being out to get you, but just trying to get your attention. What better way to flatter an artist than to draw attention to their work?" She nudged Nick who was seated next to her. "What do you think?"

"I think you may be on to something," he said, motioning to Claire. "That guy Jensen. He was a little obsessed."

Claire felt Riley tense beside her, and she recalled their conversation about Jensen at the gallery. She turned to face Riley. "I know you're fond of him, but at least consider the possibility there's a side of him you know nothing about."

Riley's expression was thoughtful, and a few beats of silence passed before she answered. "I can't see it, but I'm willing to admit I don't know him very well. Come to think of it, I don't know many people in the group very well. I mean aside from Jensen, Buster, and Natalie, I rarely see any of them outside of our meet-ups."

Claire could tell it pained Riley to think any of her art pals might have a secret, criminal life, and she was drawn to her tender heart, naive though it may be. They brainstormed for a while longer, but after a couple of glasses of tequila and over an hour talking through all the evidence they had so far, they were left with lots of questions and few conclusions. In the car on the way home, they rode in silence until they were almost to Riley's. Claire reached over and grasped Riley's hand and gently squeezed. "I could tell that was hard for you."

Riley caught her hand as she was about to draw it back and held on. "I don't like thinking the worst of people."

Claire pulled up in front of the brownstone and put the car in park. She shifted in her seat to face Riley. "Believe it or not, I don't either, even though it's kind of what I do for a living."

Riley cracked a smile. "That's inconvenient."

"It can be."

"When did you stop thinking the worst of me?"

"I don't think I ever got to that point." Claire traced Riley's palm with her fingers. "On some level, I knew you were one of the good ones."

"You did, did you?"

Riley's tone was coy, but Claire knew she wasn't a tease which meant this was genuine flirting. Suddenly, the car was very warm, and she was very warm, and she was very conscious that, despite the fact the surveillance on Riley had been called off, anyone driving or walking by had a clear view into the vehicle. Not that there was anything to see. Yet.

"Do you want to come up?" Riley asked, her voice cracking slightly.

Claire knew she shouldn't. If she went upstairs with Riley, feeling the way she felt right now, she'd be crossing a line with a witness, taking a risk with her career, but if she didn't, she knew she'd regret sacrificing her feelings for her work like she'd done every day of her life up to now. She closed her eyes and shut out the part of her brain that had run everything in her life up to this moment. When the inner voice was finally silenced, she was able to tune in to the call of her heart, and the answer came easily. "Yes. Please."

Chapter Seventeen

Riley jammed her key in the door and jerked it to the right, the task made harder by the distraction of Claire's hands on her back, winding their way up her jacket and tugging her shirt out of her jeans. She shoved her way inside her apartment, barely able to contain the urgent need to pull Claire into her arms. She shut the door behind them and whirled around, pulling Claire into her arms and shivering when Claire's hands stroked her naked back. "You're killing me."

Claire leaned back and gave her a long, slow smile. Riley dipped her head, touching her lips to Claire's, savoring the simple connection before pressing harder to deepen the kiss. Claire opened her mouth to welcome her in, and Riley moaned with pleasure as they tasted and teased in tandem. When they broke for air, Riley could barely form words, murmuring, "so good, so good." She shrugged out of her jacket and tugged the rest of her shirt from her waistband.

"Here, let me," Claire said, easing her hands around Riley's waist in slow, delicious strokes. She started unbuttoning Riley's shirt, taking her time, finally shucking it off and tossing it on the couch with her bra close behind. Claire traced her breasts, lightly rubbing her thumbs over her nipples until they peaked with desire, and then she bent and sucked each one in turn. Riley, lost in the sensation, staggered and braced against the wall, desperate not to break their embrace. Claire lavished her breasts with her tongue, over and over and over until Riley was certain she would come while standing in the center of the room.

"Do you have a bed behind that screen?" Claire whispered in her ear.

"I do," Riley gasped.

"I think we should get you into it. There are things I want to do, and if I do them right, you won't be able to stand for long."

"You might be a mind reader." Riley grasped Claire's hand and led her to the bed.

"Someone likes a lot of pillows," Claire said, grabbing one of the many throw pillows from the bed and giving a tight squeeze.

"Pillows are one of my guilty pleasures." Riley pulled her favorite patchwork velvet pillow into her arms. She rubbed her face against its soft surface. "Feels so good."

"Wishing I was a velvet pillow right now."

Riley reached out and ran her hand along the side of Claire's face. "Don't tell my pillow, but I think you're winning the 'feels so good' competition."

"Oh, there's a competition?" Claire asked. "I love a competition."

Riley grinned. "Really? I never would've guessed." She'd barely gotten the words out before Claire tugged her onto the bed.

"You won the kissing contest," Claire said, settling beneath her, propped on the giant collection of pillows. "But we have many other events to go."

As she spoke, Claire started unfastening her blouse, but Riley placed her hands over Claire's and pushed them away. "I got this. Save your energy for the next round." As she slowly loosened each button, she dropped her head and ran her tongue down the length of Claire's neck. She pulled back the silk and left a trail of whisper light kisses on Claire's naked shoulder as she unfastened her bra and slowly removed it along with the shirt, letting the delicious delay of anticipation amp up her desire.

"I want to feel every inch of you," Claire gasped, fumbling with buttons on Riley's jeans. Riley reached out with one hand and grasped the headboard, struggling to contain her arousal as

Claire slid her hand inside the waistband of her boxer briefs and inched her fingers toward her wet center. Riley's hips rocked in time with Claire's steady strokes, and she bent forward, taking one of Claire's hard nipples into her mouth and circling it with her tongue. Claire arched off the bed, and moved her hand lower, entering Riley with one finger, then two. Between thrusts, Claire's thumb glided over her clit, soft passes at first, then with mounting pressure until Riley could no longer distinguish the difference between giving pleasure and receiving it. She closed her eyes and let her only awareness be every touch between them—electric, sparking waves of ecstasy, pulsing and pounding her toward unimaginable release. When she came, she heard deep, guttural groans of pleasure, and she recognized the voice as her own though she'd never made these sounds, never experienced this level of pleasure.

A hand brushed against her cheek and she opened her eyes. She was lying next to Claire, in her arms. Safe and sated, staring at tender blue eyes looking deep into her soul. "You."

"Yes." Claire laced her fingers through hers. "Also, you. That was amazing."

"You have no idea."

"I kind of do." Claire traced her lips with her forefinger. "I had a front row seat."

Riley kissed the tip of Claire's finger. "Are we still on the competition theme?"

Claire shook her head slowly, her blond waves fanning out against her shoulder. "I think we already have a winner."

"Oh, is that right?" Riley caught her wrist and gently flipped Claire over so that she was on top for the second time. She stretched Claire's arm onto the pillow above her head and used her other hand to do the same with Claire's other arm, joining them both at the wrist with one hand. She dipped her head and brushed her lips across Claire's, pausing long enough to tease Claire into arching off the bed for more before lightly kissing her way down her chest, pausing to coax her nipples into hard points of pleasure before she dropped lower, dipping her tongue into Claire's warm, wet core, holding on tight as Claire rocked beneath her. She never would've imagined Claire surrendering to pleasure with such abandon, and it was the ultimate aphrodisiac. This woman was full of surprises and she planned to spend the rest of the night teasing them out of her.

❖

Claire rolled onto her side and patted the bed beside her. Nothing. She opened her eyes and scanned what she could see without sitting up—she wasn't sure she had the energy after a full night in Riley's bed. She was still there, but Riley wasn't, and the idea of waking up without her after the night they'd shared left her lonely and a little sad.

"You're awake."

Claire turned her head at the sound of Riley's voice and pulled a muscle. "Ouch," she said, rubbing her neck. The pain was worth it. Riley stood next to the bed wearing tight jeans and an even tighter black T-shirt that hugged her sculpted chest. That beautiful body had topped her well into the night.

Riley grinned as if she could tell what Claire was thinking and set a steaming cup on the nightstand. Claire sniffed the air. "Is that coffee?"

"It is. I borrowed it from the couple downstairs. I hope it's good. They fancy themselves to be quote the 'in-home baristas,' and they used lots of fancy words to describe its 'essence.'"

Claire held the cup to her lips and let the aroma surround her before taking a sip. She moaned and took another.

"I recognize that sound," Riley said. "Although you weren't drinking coffee the last time you made it."

"Coffee is now my second favorite thing," Claire said. She reached for Riley's hand. "A distant second."

Riley bent down and cupped the back of her neck, gently pulling her into a slow, deep kiss, before settling in next to her in bed. "Last night was unexpected, but it was amazing."

"Any regrets?" Claire asked.

"None. You?"

Claire saw the hopeful expression in Riley's eyes and she fought hesitation. In this moment she wasn't having any second thoughts, but that's how it worked when you were basking in the glow. Would the flurry of emotions that accompanied this incredible attraction have staying power when she was back in the real world where cops weren't supposed to sleep with witnesses and everyone was a suspect until the case was closed? She didn't know the answer, but right now a gorgeous woman who'd spent the night pleasing her had wandered out to find her drink of choice in an incredibly thoughtful gesture, and she owed her an expression of appreciation. "Remember how I said any gallery would be lucky to have you?"

"Yes."

"Any woman would be lucky to have you too. Your art extends beyond the canvas."

"I'd say I bet you say that to all the girls," Riley said, "But maybe you don't date a lot of artists."

"I speak the truth, but you'd be right. I don't date much of anyone. Job tends to get in the way. Most women don't understand why I have to keep rushing off in the night or they assume I'm using the job as a cover for cheating."

"Trust is important. Both ways."

"Agreed," Claire said. "How about you? Date much?"

Riley shook her head. "I get to the second or third date before they start asking questions about family. The whole dad's in prison thing is either a nonstarter or they're morbidly curious about the details of murder trials and prison life, and they quickly lose interest when they realize I'm an expert at neither."

"That sucks."

"It does, but it's part of my story, for better or worse." Riley stroked her shoulder. "Right now, I guess you could say I'm reaping the benefits."

And just like that, Claire's hesitation disappeared. She set her coffee down and turned into Riley's arms, ready to resume their electric connection, but a loud buzzing jarred her out of the moment. "Is that—"

Riley reached over to the nightstand and handed over her phone. "It was on the floor this morning. Must've fallen out of your pocket during the clothes shedding portion of the evening."

Claire took it from her hand with a sense of dread that the real world was about to burst their bubble. She was right.

You and Redding. My office. Nine a.m. sharp.

The only other time she'd been ordered to appear before her squad commander, Major Reggie Holland, on short notice, she'd received a commendation, but she knew in her gut this wasn't that. Shit. She texted Nick to give him a heads-up and told him she'd meet him at the station. When she finished typing, she looked up from her phone. Riley was staring at her with a wistful expression.

"You have to go."

"I do."

Riley smiled. "This is when all those other women would bail on you, right?"

"You make it sound like there's been a whole bunch of other women." Claire shook her head. "There hasn't, but yes, that's the way it usually works."

Riley leaned over and kissed her cheek. "Let's change that pattern. You go do your work and I'll do mine. When we're both done, let's find each other and do this," she motioned to the bed, "again. Okay?"

Claire studied Riley's face, looking for any sign she was annoyed about her imminent departure, but she saw nothing but kindness and caring, laced with a trace of longing, which was entirely different from the resentment she was used to from other women. "That sounds perfect."

Chapter Eighteen

Claire pulled up to the station and parked, but before she exited her vehicle, she closed her eyes for a moment and imagined she was back at Riley's apartment, curled against her body, resting before another bout of making love.

Whoa. Making love? Where had those words come from? She rephrased the thought in her head as "having sex," but the term didn't begin to describe the intimacy she'd shared with Riley. Their closeness had been steadily growing, and whatever she chose to name last night's activity, it couldn't be reduced to a mere physical act. She liked Riley, that was for sure, but were her feelings deeper still?

Claire filed the internal debate away, determined to examine it later, when she wasn't distracted by this case and whatever it was her boss wanted this morning. The real challenge would be focusing on the investigation with visions of Riley's naked body on a continuous reel in her head.

When she entered the building, she spotted Nick in the lobby. "Good morning. Thanks for hosting last night. I had a great time."

"You must have because you seem unusually happy this morning." He pulled her aside. "Cheryl thinks you went home with Riley last night. Tell me you're not that crazy."

Claire averted her eyes before she could stop herself even though she knew it would confirm his suspicions. "I'm not crazy, but let's agree not to talk about Riley. I don't want to fight with you. We need to stick together right now."

Nick sighed. "Fine. United front for the boss, but at some point, we need to discuss what's going on. Any idea why we're getting hauled in this morning?"

"I hope it's because Holland is forming a task force and wants us to lead it," Claire said.

"I hear a but…"

"But I have a feeling we're going to get chewed out for not solving this case before the third body showed up."

A few minutes later, they were standing outside Major Holland's office. Through the closed door, they could hear raised voices, and Claire was certain she recognized one of them. When the door finally opened, her suspicion was confirmed. Bruce was standing to the side of her commander's desk, his face red and his expression agitated. "Chief Kehler," Claire said, easily assuming the formality expected in public. "Good to see you, sir." She turned to her squad commander. "Major Holland, nice to see you too."

Holland shook her head. "You'll probably change your mind about that before you leave here." She pointed to the chairs in front of her desk. "Sit."

"What the hell's going on?" Bruce bellowed. "Three dead bodies? Are you ready to make an arrest? I've got the mayor's office, the county commissioners, and every other bastard with pull in this town breathing down my neck. The chief is asking if we need to bring in the feds, but I told him my people are capable of solving crimes without having their hands held. Was I wrong?"

Claire flicked a glance at Nick to let him know she would respond, and he answered with a slight nod. "You weren't wrong. We're making progress." She walked him through their investigation so far, including their interviews with the members of the Eastside Sketchers. "We have a couple of potential people of interest in the group," she said, referring to Buster and Jensen, "and we're taking a closer look."

"Unless one of them is Riley Flynn, you're wasting your time. She and Frank Flynn should be your prime suspects. Didn't you say Riley confessed that the drawings were hers?"

Claire's gut wrenched at his deliberate twisting of the facts. She took a deep breath and slowly let it go before responding. "Yes, the sketches are hers. But she has a solid alibi for at least one of the murders, and we have nothing to tie Frank Flynn to the case."

"Other than the fact, these murders started weeks after his release and there are strong similarities in the MO," Bruce said. "For all you know, he's leaving her sketches at the murder scenes in some kind of weird father-daughter connection. Have you even given him a hard look?"

They hadn't, but for good reasons, but reasons Claire was hesitant to point out when it was clear Bruce had an irrational attachment to tagging Riley's dad with these crimes. If Nick were here alone, he would probably speak up in defense of their decision not to focus on Frank Flynn, but he was in a completely different position than she was. Bruce wasn't his mentor, with powerful sway over her career. And he hadn't slept with Riley last night, an act that Bruce would surely deem a clear detriment to her subjectivity. There was only one solution. Take a closer look at Frank Flynn. If he did commit the murders, he deserved to be punished. If he didn't, then they could check another suspect off their list and move on.

"We'll take a closer look," she said, purposefully not looking in Nick's direction. She'd be able to explain her decision later, when they weren't standing in front of their superiors. For now, she needed to get Bruce off her back, so they could solve this case their way.

"Great," Bruce said, his anger dissipating into a self-satisfied smile. "Glad we're on the same page."

Major Holland gave them a rundown of the resources the department was making available to the investigation in terms of personnel, etc., and dismissed them to get back to work. Claire led Nick out of the office.

"What was that all about?" he whispered. "And why did you—"

She placed a finger over her lips. "Let's ride together and catch up then," she said, hoping he'd follow her lead and hold off talking about this until they were sure they were alone. Her instincts were spot-on because at that moment, Bruce called out to her.

"Detective Hanlon, a word."

She told Nick to meet her in the lobby and she walked back toward Bruce who pulled her into an empty conference room and shut the door.

"I thought you wanted this promotion," Bruce said. "People don't get promotions by being nice. It's time for you to make some hard calls. You feel sorry for this girl because her dad's a killer? Your sympathy would be better spent on the three women he may have killed. Explain your reservations to their families, or better yet, make an arrest and give their families some closure. If Flynn says he has an alibi, I want it turned inside out. If there are any holes in his story, arrest him. His hearing's on Monday and if the judge rules in his favor, the press he'll get will make him untouchable. You have until then to make a case and I want twice-daily reports on the progress you've made between now and then. Understood?"

She did. He expected them to work all weekend until they found something, anything, to tie Frank Flynn to the murders. She'd put in the hours, but at the end of the weekend, if the evidence didn't point to Frank, she wasn't going to pretend it did. Until then, she'd let Bruce think she was doing everything in her power to fulfill his prophecy as long as he didn't hurt Riley in the process.

❖

Riley tore another sheet out of her sketchpad and crumpled it into a ball.

"That's the third one," said Jensen. "Not feeling it today?"

"Guess not," she said. She'd set up between him and Warren outside of the Shed at the Dallas Farmer's Market for the last hour, and the rest of the Eastside Sketchers were scattered around the market. Unlike the others, Riley had nothing to show for her efforts, and not for lack of subject matter. On a Saturday, the market was bustling with both locals and tourists, but unlike all the other times she'd come here to draw, this time she was completely uninspired.

She knew why even if she didn't want to admit it. She'd let Claire get too close too quickly, and when Claire had texted this afternoon to say she couldn't make it to the meet-up, her inspiration drained away.

Riley picked up her phone and read the screen again, looking for some deeper meaning behind Claire's message. *Things are heating up at work. Will text you when I'm free.* Had the text not come on the heels of a similar one on Friday night, she might have taken it at face value, but Claire blowing her off twice within twenty-four hours of the most intimate night of her life made Riley question whether she'd been misreading the signals Claire had been sending all along.

When had she become the kind of person who got attached, staring at her phone, looking for crumbs of affection between the sparse words in a text message? She'd never let anyone else get this close and her current state of aggravation told her that had been a solid plan. Maybe it was true that Claire had to work, and sure, Riley had said she wasn't the clingy sort, but she couldn't help but feel the first tender moments of any relationship were fragile, deserving a little more attention than a few words of text.

Hell, what did she know? It wasn't like she'd been in a relationship before. And it wasn't like Claire was ghosting her. She wished she had someone to talk to, but Buster and Natalie had tickets to a concert after the meet-up, and she wasn't in the mood to spill her heart out to any of the others over drinks at the Ginger Man.

Jensen tapped her on the shoulder. "No shame in bailing if you're not feeling it."

"Let her be," Warren said with a gentle smile. "She might want to channel some of that aggravation into her art."

"It's an urbanscape, not a Munch," Jensen said. "What's she going to do, draw ominous clouds and everyone screaming?"

Riley waved her pencil in the air. "Truce, you two. I appreciate the concern, but it's true, I'm just having an off day." She started packing her bag. "I'm going to head out."

"If you're still not feeling it tomorrow, we can cancel," Jensen said.

Riley paused for a moment, and then she remembered. She'd promised to meet him at his place and walk to one of her favorite spots at the lake to catch the sunset. She wanted to take him up on his offer to cancel, but walking around the lake might be the perfect antidote to her current mood. "No, let's do it. I'll meet you at your place around four thirty."

"Perfection," Jensen said.

On a normal day, she'd respond in kind, but she could only manage a wave as she left the group and headed back to her car for the short ride back to her place. When she pulled up in front of the brownstone, her phone buzzed, and she grabbed it and stared at the screen. She didn't recognize the number, but thinking Claire could be calling from work, she answered anyway. "Hello?"

"Riley, it's Morgan Bradley."

It took her a moment to register it was her father's attorney calling. "Uh, hi. What can I do for you?"

"I don't mean to bother you, but your father just sent me a text that Detective Hanlon and her partner came by his house today. I remembered you mentioned Detective Hanlon had come to talk to you as well, and I wanted to find out if she's been in touch with you."

Riley stared out the window, unsure how to respond. Yes, Claire had been in touch with her, but not in the way Morgan was talking about, and no way was she giving details about her relationship with Claire to a virtual stranger. But Claire had mentioned her father earlier in the week. The night of the third murder when Claire had shown up at her house. She'd said that Frank hadn't been home that night, but Claire hadn't pressed past the implication that Frank had had the opportunity to commit the crime, and she hadn't brought it up Thursday night during their brainstorming session with Nick and Cheryl. Maybe Claire's visit to Frank today was simply to check off a box before moving on with the investigation, and she said as much to Morgan.

"That could be true," Morgan replied. "My trust level is pretty low when it comes to the police talking to your father. They don't exactly have a good track record where he's concerned."

Riley started to protest. To say, "But this is Claire. She's honorable and her only goal is to find the truth. She's not like those other cops." But if Morgan asked how she'd come to these characterizations, she wasn't prepared to answer without divulging the depth of her feelings and risking putting Claire's objectivity under a microscope. "I don't know what they're up to," she said—an honest, yet incomplete answer.

"Okay. Well, I'm sorry to bug you on a Saturday. Any chance you've changed your mind about attending the hearing on Monday?"

"I haven't decided," Riley didn't try to curb the edge in her voice. "I doubt I'll decide until right before it happens."

"Fair enough. Do whatever's right for you. For what it's worth, no matter what the judge says, everyone in my firm believes he's innocent."

After she ended the call, Riley went up to her apartment, set the kettle on for tea, and dug out the file full of motions Morgan had given her. It was thick and the language in the documents was stiff and formal, but Riley spent the next few hours reading every word. By the time she reached the end, she was convinced Morgan was right. Her father's conviction was a combination of unfortunate circumstances, shoddy police work, and a rush to judgment.

But if he was innocent of Linda Bradshaw's murder, why was Claire questioning him about these new cases? Granted, she didn't know all of the facts of the new cases, but it looked like the only similarities were the race and ages of the female victims. And didn't it stand to reason that if he wasn't guilty of the original case involving a white, twenty-something woman, then there was nothing left to link him to these current crimes?

A knock on her door startled her out of her focus. She walked to the door, hoping it wasn't one of the neighbors needing her services—the coeds downstairs had a habit of locking themselves out on the weekend. The knocking grew more intense as she closed the distance, bolstering her suspicions, and she called out, "On my way."

She opened the door without looking first, convinced she was right about the neighbors, but she was wrong. It was Claire standing on her doorstep, looking tired and sad and delicious all at the same time. Riley had never been happier to be wrong.

Nick edged in front of Claire and she let him. Frank Flynn wasn't a big guy, but he sported the kind of muscles someone got when all they had to do with their free time was work out in the prison gym. He was standing in his doorway, blocking their view inside, and a dog was barking furiously from somewhere behind him. Nick flashed his shield. "I'm Detective Redding and this is Detective Hanlon. Are you Frank Flynn?"

"I find it hard to believe you don't already know who I am. Don't you people have a bull's-eye with my face on it at your headquarters?"

"Mr. Flynn, we'd like to talk to you for a moment," Claire asked, ignoring his remark. "May we come inside?"

"No, you may not."

She tried a different tack. "Then could you step out here?"

He shook his head. "Let me be clear. If you want to talk to me, you can call my attorney."

"We're not here to talk to you about your pending case," Nick chimed in.

"My attorney. Call her."

Claire recognized the mantra of someone who'd been through the system, but she couldn't resist one last question. "Is that your dog?" Claire asked, leaning to the right in an attempt to see the canine.

"My attorney's name is Morgan Bradley. Would you like her phone number?"

Claire shook her head at Nick, and they walked back to her car. "Well, that was a bust," she said as they drove away.

"He has a dog."

"We don't even know if it's his," Claire said. "Besides, I thought you were firmly on the Frank Flynn was wronged side."

"He was. For what happened in the past, but right now, we don't have much else to go on. I'll take a break wherever we can find it."

"I hear you, but that's a leap. Lots of people have dogs."

"I know," he said. "Are you headed back to the station?"

"No, I can no longer stare at files full of disjointed information unless I'm in the comfort of my own home. Let's call it a night and start back tomorrow. I'll take you home."

A few minutes later, she pulled up in front of Nick's house. "You want to come in for some of Cheryl's outrageously expensive tequila?" he asked.

Claire wavered for a moment. "Better not. I still need to send a report to Bruce. A few sips of that stuff and I'll forget why I wanted to be a detective in the first place."

"Tell you what. You go home and get some rest and I'll send tonight's report. You get the next one."

Normally, she'd wave off the offer, but she wasn't sure she was in any condition to write a coherent report. "Thanks. Make sure to make it clear he refused to talk to us and invoked counsel."

"Will do."

She watched him walk to the door and smiled when Cheryl poked her head out and waved. What would it be like to come home at the end of a grueling day to someone who loved you, and when had she started wondering about things like that?

She didn't know the answer, but she did know that she didn't want to end this day without seeing Riley, if only for a few minutes. She drove straight to the brownstone and took the stairs to Riley's apartment two at a time, praying her idea to surprise Riley instead of calling first wouldn't fall flat. When Riley opened the door, her expression was guarded, and Claire wondered if she miscalculated her chance of a welcome.

"Surprise," she said. "I know I should've called, but it's been a helluva day, and all I could think about was how much I wanted to see you before it ends. But now I'm thinking maybe that was a bad idea. You don't look particularly happy to see me."

"Wrong." Riley stepped aside. "Come in."

Claire followed her into the room, but when Riley suggested they sit, she begged off. "I can't stay long."

"Okay."

"You seem annoyed."

"Did you go to my dad's house today?" Riley asked.

"Did he tell you we came by?"

"Don't do that."

"Do what?" Claire asked, certain she knew what Riley meant, but desperate to keep her distance for now.

"Answer a question with a question instead of answering what was asked. You're doing it to deflect." Riley reached for her hand and Claire didn't back away from the touch. "I thought we were past that," she said, her voice now soft and gentle.

"Riley, this is my job. I can't tell you everything." She watched sadness fill Riley's eyes and she instantly regretted the harshness of her tone. "Not yet."

"Okay. I get it. The civilian has been sidelined."

"It's not that simple." Claire wanted to tell Riley that her boss was out to get her father, but what was the point of getting her worked up about it? There was no evidence to link Frank Flynn to these crimes, and eventually Bruce would see that. The best thing she could do for Riley was go home, review all the evidence again, and figure out why someone had tangled her up in this mess. She looked down at their joined hands. It wasn't the same as coming home to someone at the end of the day, but their connection was a start, the beginning of something bigger. She could feel it and she knew Riley did too. All she had to do was solve this case, and she'd be free to explore these new feelings.

"I promise, this will all be over soon. Until then, I have to focus." She grinned. "And it's pretty damn hard to focus with you in the room." She leaned in and captured Riley's lips between her own in a soft, lingering kiss. "I'll call you tomorrow," she promised as she left, quickly before she could change her mind.

Chapter Nineteen

If we don't eat something soon, my brain will melt right inside of my skull," Nick said with a groan, dramatically slumping down in his chair.

Claire threw a paper airplane she'd made from one of the index cards they'd been using to track the evidence in the case at his head. "That doesn't even make sense."

He pointed at the whiteboard on the wall. "It makes about as much sense as your flowchart to nowhere."

He was right. They'd spent all morning reviewing every piece of evidence they had. Interview notes from each victim's family, friends, and co-workers and members of the Eastside Sketchers, Reyes's autopsy reports, photographs of the scene, and they were no closer to any conclusions than they'd been when they started. The best idea she'd had was to run full background checks on every one of the Eastside Sketchers who'd been at the Old Red meet-up when Riley's sketchbook had gone missing, and they were still waiting on the results.

"I'll feed you if you come up with one new idea," she said. "Something that will get Bruce to move off his obsession with Frank Flynn."

Nick suddenly sat up straight. He jerked his chin toward the glass door of the conference room. "Speak of the devil," he whispered.

Claire turned to see Bruce walking toward them, a sheaf of papers in his hand. He pushed through the door of the room and tossed the papers on the table.

"You're welcome," he said.

Claire was almost afraid to ask. She pulled the papers toward her and read the first page. "A search warrant for Frank Flynn's house?"

"Yes. Signed by Judge Richter. There's a team on standby to help you execute the search. Are you ready?"

Claire looked at Nick and widened her eyes to telegraph her surprise. She flipped to the affidavit and skimmed the text of the document supporting the warrant. Under Bruce's impatient stare, she was only able to glean a few key phrases here and there—dog hairs, daughter's sketches, silk scarves. It read like Bruce had compiled a list of the forensic evidence at each scene and then bootstrapped an argument asserting that because of Frank's past and his current association with Riley, there must be similar evidence where he lived. The arguments were thin, but the judge's signature was all they needed to make the warrant official, and Judge Richter was well known for his propensity to side with the police when there was any doubt.

"Chief, may I speak with you alone for a moment?" Claire asked, hoping Nick would read her mind. She needn't have worried. He excused himself to the john, and as soon as he'd cleared the door of the conference room, she turned to confront Bruce as a mentor, not her superior, but he spoke first.

"I know what you're going to say. Richter would sign a blank check if we brought it to him, but this is a gift. Instead of spinning your wheels, you get to do some actual police work."

"I don't feel right about this. Part of the basis for the warrant is a dog we heard barking at the house. We didn't even see the dog and we don't know who it belongs to or how long it's been living there, but we're supposed to collect hairs and send them out to be tested?"

"You didn't have any problem grabbing a few hairs off Buster Creel's dog." He grinned. "Yes, I've been reading your reports."

"We were invited into Buster's house. This is different."

He pointed at the warrant. "*This* is how you lead. That promotion isn't going to happen if you can't step up. Can I count on you?"

She stared at the warrant like it was a coiled snake ready to deliver poison. And it would if Frank was smart enough to hire a good attorney to challenge it in court. But what if he had a Lionel Darby on his side and what if they found real evidence that helped them close this case before any other young women were murdered? Was a sense of loyalty to Riley more important than preventing another murder?

She knew Bruce was going to have this warrant executed whether she led the team or not. At least if she was in charge, she could make sure they adhered to the letter of the law if not the spirit. She didn't know how that would go over with Riley, but she had to trust their connection would survive because for the first time in her life, personal sacrifice—in the form of Riley shutting her out—wasn't worth professional gain.

Sunday morning, Riley deliberately placed her phone across the room to keep from checking it for messages from Claire. She was preparing for next week's classes, and the distraction of wondering what Claire was doing was bad enough without the added frustration of picking up her phone every few minutes only to find Claire hadn't reached out because her focus was elsewhere.

Her apartment was so quiet that when the phone finally did ring, she jumped at the sound. With four long strides, she crossed the room and looked at the screen. The number was familiar, but it wasn't Claire's. She took a chance and answered it anyway. "Hello?"

"Riley, it's Parker Casey, Morgan Bradley's law partner."

"Listen, I told Morgan yesterday that I'd think about going to the hearing, but I haven't made my decision."

"That's not why I'm calling. In fact, I'm not sure there's going to be a hearing."

"Oh." Riley sank onto the couch, certain hearing from her father's attorneys two days in a row couldn't be a good thing. "What's going on?"

"DPD is in the process of serving a search warrant at your father's house in connection with the recent murder cases around town that you discussed with Morgan. She's on her way over there now, but she wanted me to give you a heads-up in case the police show up at your place."

"Why would they show up here?"

"If you repeat this, I'll deny it, but one of my buddies on the force said that the search warrant affidavit—that's the information the judge relies on to give them permission to search—references sketches of yours that were found on the murder victims. It's entirely possible you might be next on their list."

Riley wanted to tell Parker she was wrong. That she'd been cooperating with the investigation and Claire had already cleared her as a potential suspect. But a nagging feeling crept up her spine, urging her to find out more before she opened her mouth. "Thanks for the warning. I have to go." She hung up before Parker could respond and immediately fired off a text to Claire.

Are you arresting my father?

She set the phone down and stared at it, willing it to come to life with words of reassurance. For a full sixty seconds—she counted—there was nothing, and then dots appeared to indicate Claire was typing her response. Finally, her message appeared on the screen. *No. Can't talk now. Hang tight.*

Hang tight? What the hell kind of platitude was that? She was tight, all right. She was twisted in knots at the idea of the police storming her home and shoving their way through her studio, exposing her unfinished work to strangers. She typed her response so fast, she had to retype it three times before she got the question right. *Do you have a warrant for my apartment?*

Again, the interminable wait before finally the answer appeared. *No.* That was it. No explanation, nothing more to put her at ease. She wasn't sure what she'd expected. Claire was on the job and what Riley had suspected from the beginning and brushed aside in the name of attraction was becoming clear. Cop Claire was a very different person from the woman who'd shared her bed. And of course she was. Her entire life revolved around her career; she'd said so herself. But Riley had ignored the signs because she'd wanted to believe the tender woman who'd made love to her was a bigger part of the whole than this version of Claire whose singular focus was closing this case.

She waited another few minutes before deciding Claire's last message was the end of the conversation. She tossed her phone into her bag along with a new sketchbook and a box of her favorite pencils. She'd considered canceling on Jensen, but now she really needed the distraction.

She drove the long way around the lake, past the spillway, and the arboretum, feeling her mind and body relax at the soothing sight of joggers and cyclists enjoying the last rays of daylight before dusk settled in over the water. She turned into Jensen's apartment complex, envying its proximity to the water's edge as she had when she'd been here once before. If she didn't have a deal with the landlord at the brownstone, she'd want to live here where she could step outside and be in nature within moments. She found a parking space marked visitor, scooped up her bag, and headed toward Jensen's building.

"Riley!"

She turned at the sound of her name, shielding her eyes against the sun as she tried to find the source of the voice.

"Over here," the voice called out.

The voice was deeper than Jensen's, and for a moment she thought one of her students had spotted her and wanted to say hello. She walked through the parking lot, toward the sound, surprised when Warren Spencer stepped out from behind a large SUV. "Hey, Warren."

"Hi," he said. "Bet you didn't expect to see me here." Before she could answer, he added, "Jensen invited me to tag along. Hope you don't mind."

"Of course not." Given her current mood, she would've preferred a one-on-one lesson today, but maybe teaching the two of them would provide added distraction from thoughts about Claire. "I told Jensen I'd knock on his door when I got here."

"Me too," Warren said. He swept his arm in a flourish toward the building. "After you."

Riley smiled at the old-fashioned gesture and took the lead. They'd only gone a few steps when he called out. She looked back and he was staring at his phone. "What's up?"

"Jensen just sent me a text to say he's on campus and his car won't start." He started typing into his phone.

Riley instinctively pulled out her own phone to check for a similar text, but the last text she'd received had been the one from Claire earlier today.

"He said he was about to text you, but I let him know we're together. I asked him if he needs help, but he said no. He's waiting on a friend who lives on campus that might be able to get his car running. He's not going to make it back before sunset though."

"That's all right," Riley said, feeling a twinge of relief. "We can reschedule."

"Oh, okay," Warren said, his voice laced with disappointment. "I'm sure you have better things to do with your spare time than giving an old amateur like me some pointers."

Riley looked up at the sun, which was dropping lower in the sky. As if he read her mind, Warren said, "We can drive over to the boat slip and get there in time to set up before the sun crests over the water's edge."

Riley imagined the scene full of oranges and blues and purples, playing out against the water, and decided a burst of nature was exactly what she needed right now. "Let's do it, but I can drive." She started to reach for her keys, but Warren jingled his in front of her and pointed at the SUV next to them.

"Please let me." He patted the side of the vehicle and pressed the button on the remote to unlock the doors. "Hop in."

Riley climbed into the passenger side and settled into the cushy leather seat. She surveyed the dashboard and determined it had every optional feature available. "Sweet ride," she said to Warren as he settled into the driver's seat.

"Isn't it?" He smiled, while he fumbled with something on his left. "I'm still learning the features." He pointed to the shoulder belt. "Speaking of which, that will be easier to fasten if you do this." He leaned closer and reached across her chest as if to grab the belt, but the next thing she knew she couldn't see. With her right hand, she reached for whatever was covering her eyes, but intense pressure against her neck drew her attention away. It became difficult to swallow and she lowered her hand, slapping out against whatever was choking her, but she couldn't gain purchase. Adrenaline surged through her, and she thrashed against the pressure, the panic only making the pain more intense. The last thing she remembered before she passed out was the smell of chloroform and the fear of death.

Chapter Twenty

Claire knocked on Riley's door for the third time when she heard a door open downstairs.

"She's not home," a woman's voice called out.

Claire peered over the railing at the twenty-something sporting a beret. She bet this was the coffee lending neighbor, and she took a chance she might be equally as generous with information. "We were supposed to meet here. Do you happen to know where she went?"

Beret cocked her head like she was thinking. "Not sure, but she had the bag she takes when she goes out to draw."

"Thanks." Claire stood on the landing contemplating her next move. She wanted to go home and shower and eat and sleep, but she knew none of those things would be fulfilling until she talked to Riley and explained what had gone down today. They'd served the warrant and found a whole lot of nothing. The dog wasn't there when they showed up, and Frank's roommate told them it was his sister's and he'd only been keeping it for a few days. Bruce had still insisted they send dog hairs they found in the house to Reyes for testing, and he'd talked the DA into filing a motion to delay Frank's hearing pending the outcome. Claire wanted Riley to hear about it from her first, but she'd have to find her to make that happen.

She was walking back to her car, when her phone buzzed. She looked at the screen, hoping it was Riley, but it was Nick. "Hey, what's up?"

"Probably nothing, but that Jensen guy just called me. It was kind of weird. He said he was supposed to meet up with Riley today at his place for an art lesson, but she stood him up."

Claire knew how he felt. "So? She's an adult. If she decides to blow him off, I'm not sure what we're supposed to do about that."

"That's the thing. He said her SUV is parked at his apartment complex. She was supposed to meet him there and they were going to the boat slip together. Something about sketching the sunset on the water. He sent her a few texts, but she hasn't responded. I guess she decided to go on her own, but I figured I should let you know. You want me to go by there and check it out?"

"No, I'm not home yet. I'll go by." Claire told herself it was probably nothing. She fired off a text to Riley and turned in the direction of the lake. The car Jensen had seen was probably one that looked like Riley's or Riley had decided to go to the boat slip alone. Still, she zipped toward her destination, grateful for the light weekend traffic. When she reached Jensen's apartment complex, she slowed down and cruised the parking lot, looking for Riley's SUV. She spotted it on her first pass, parked in a visitor's spot. She touched the hood and it was cool. She circled the car, scouting for any signs of foul play, but there was nothing to indicate anything other than Riley had left her car parked here without incident.

The simplest explanation was that Riley had walked down to the boat slip on her own, but Jensen had been so certain they'd had plans, he'd called Nick to report that Riley hadn't shown up. Riley didn't strike her as the kind of person who'd no-show on a friend, and Claire sensed something was off. She pulled out her phone. Riley hadn't responded to her first text, but she fired off another anyway, staring at the screen after she hit send, praying for a quick response. When the phone rang in her hand, it almost startled her into dropping it.

"Hey, Nick. I just got here. Her car's here, but no sign of her. Any word from Jensen?"

"No, he was going to head down to the boat slip to see if she was there, but I told him to wait for you. I just wanted to give you a heads-up. We just got those background checks back from Lexis. Nothing out of the ordinary on Jensen, but we got several hits on that older guy Warren Spencer. His daughter, the one we saw in the wedding photos at his house? She was murdered about a year after she got married. Bruce and Danny were the detectives on the case, but it went cold."

"Okay. That's unfortunate, but I'm not sure how it relates to these murders."

"I'm not sure it does, but Warren gave interviews to several news outlets at the time of Frank Flynn's trial. The MO in his daughter's death was almost exactly the same as Linda Bradshaw. He was convinced Flynn killed Amy—that's his daughter—and he was pissed Flynn was never charged in Amy's death."

Claire gripped the phone, convinced Nick was on to something. "You said the case went cold. They never charged anyone?"

"Nope. And Warren was real sore about it at the time. Just think how angry he might be after all these years."

"Especially, when he sees Frank has a daughter who's alive and well." Claire started walking toward Jensen's apartment, as a sour dread coursed through her. "It's no coincidence Warren joined the Eastside Sketchers. I bet he wanted to get close to Riley." Which is exactly what she wanted to do, as quickly as possible. "I'll call you back." She beat on Jensen's door with her fist, not caring if his neighbors thought she was being obnoxious. She raised her hand to knock again, but the door opened before she could connect, and she almost fell forward at the momentum. Jensen held an arm to steady her.

"She hasn't shown up," he said before she could ask. "I know it's silly of me to worry. I know she's slightly older than those women who've been murdered, but I figured it was better to tell you and let you decide if I'm overreacting. I honestly didn't expect you to come down here."

Claire wanted to strangle him by the time he paused, and she blurted out her question before he could say more. "Who else knows you were meeting her today?"

Jensen looked confused at the question. "No one. I mean, no one I know of." He tapped his chin. "Wait a minute. Warren was sketching right next to us when we made our plans, but—"

Claire's insides turned to ice at the sound of Warren's name and she cut Jensen off. "Have you sketched at the boat slip before?"

"Yes, a couple of times. Riley likes this little spot by the old filter building." He fished his phone out of this pocket and started thumbing through photos. "I've got a picture of the view from there."

She tossed him a card, already on the move. "Cell number's on the back. Text it to me. Now. Tell Nick that's where I went."

"I can come with you."

"No. Call Nick." Claire dashed to her car and sped out of the parking lot and onto Garland Road, resisting the urge to pull out her lights and siren. One of two things was happening. Either Riley was sketching a sunset on the side of the lake or Warren Spencer was exacting some kind of twisted revenge. She knew in her gut it was the latter, and her best chance of stopping him would be the element of surprise. She turned right on the road on the other side of the spillway and navigated her way toward the boat slip, parking well back from the lake to walk the rest of the way to the filter building and checking to make sure her gun was loaded before she stepped out of the car and started walking toward the water.

Her phone buzzed and she slipped behind a tree. She turned the sound off and pulled up Jensen's text with the photo of the view he'd promised. She could see why Riley preferred this particular spot, it was tucked away from the walking and biking trails, yet it provided a full panorama of the sun's colors kissing the lake. She drew closer, treading softly, praying she'd find Riley sitting by the water, sketching the beautiful view and wishing she'd taken the time today to tell her she couldn't stop thinking about her, not in the context of a case, but about how Riley made her feel like a different person. Like a whole person who was allowed to want a life beyond the badge, and a lover to share it with. But not just any lover. Claire wanted Riley with her special way of seeing so much beauty in a world in which she often saw only ugliness. Riley, the tender lover, who stirred feelings in her she thought she'd never have.

Bruce could take his promotion and shove it if she could just find Riley safe and sound.

❖

Riley woke to the sound of water lapping against the shore. She was sitting on the grass, her back to the water, with her hands bound behind her and her feet tied at the ankles. Her throat was tight and sore, her head hurt, and she was nauseous, but all of that seemed trivial in comparison to the gun pointed at her face.

"You're awake," Warren said. "Good."

She tried to speak, to ask him what was going on, but a croak was all that came out. He shook the gun. "Don't bother. There's nothing you have to say that I want to hear. I hear enough of it from your pals Jensen and Buster. 'Riley is such a great teacher. Riley has her own art show.'" He scowled. "You have no idea how lucky you are to be alive."

Once again, she tried to talk, desperate to ask what was going on, but even more desperate to cry for help. She concentrated on blurting out a one-word question, settling on "What?" It sounded more like "ut," but he seemed to understand.

"My Amy was robbed of the ability to live her life to the fullest and you're about to find out what that's like. I only regret that your father isn't here to see me take from him what he took from me."

Riley wondered if he'd hit her in the head, because nothing he said made any sense, but he didn't seem to care if she understood. He started circling her, looking at her from different angles as if she were a model he was about to sketch. On his third pass, her haze gave way to realization. She didn't know why, but she knew he'd stolen her drawings and left them on the bodies of the women he'd killed. Panic pulsed through her and she forced herself to breathe slowly. She had to think clearly, or she would be his fourth victim. Any minute, he might snap, and her life would be over—no good-byes to her friends, no gallery debut, no Claire. Her story couldn't end like this, especially not when she'd just discovered what it was like to let another person in. The scary roller coaster of emotions that came from being vulnerable enough to experience falling in love. Falling in love—words she never thought she'd say about herself, but now that she'd allowed the feeling to surface, she knew that's what was happening with Claire, and that's why everything Claire did affected her so deeply.

She saw Warren backing up farther and holding up his hands as if to frame her in his sight. No, her story couldn't end like this. She had to fight for her life, for the chance to love and be loved. For Claire.

"Warren Spencer, put the gun down."

Claire. Riley snapped her head to the right searching for a sign of her in the brush. When she caught Warren watching her, she shifted to the left to try to throw him off. It didn't work. He trained his weapon in the direction where Claire's voice had sounded.

"Go away or I'll kill her."

"I have a feeling you're going to try and kill her anyway, so I think I'll stay right here."

Riley smiled. She hadn't expected Claire to be deterred by a madman, but she was determined to help. She wrestled against the rope that held her in place.

"Stop that," Warren shouted as he closed the distance between them. "You're messing up the scene." He whirled around, pointing the gun at her, at the trees, and back at her. "Stop moving."

He was too close to her now. She needed to get him to move farther away. She cleared her throat and struggled to speak. "Okay, but I need something to lean on." She nodded toward a thick tree branch lying several feet away. "Put that behind my back."

He laughed. "Right." He bent down and yanked the rope binding her wrists. Out of the corner of her eye, Riley could make out a shadow moving through the trees and prayed it was Claire coming toward them, but she'd have to act right now to give Claire a clean shot. Warren's hand was still on the rope and she jerked her hands out of his grasp and simultaneously pushed up from the ground, launching her body backward and toppling him over with a loud thud.

He clawed at her back, trying to shove her away, but she kept up the awkward assault, digging in her heels and pushing back against him, determined to keep him off his feet. She felt him scramble for purchase and she heard a metal click and remembered his gun. Claire should show up to save her any second, but quicker than that she might be dead for reasons she still didn't understand. Her life couldn't end like this, full of unspoken truths. She needed more time. Time to heal her relationship with her father. Time to tell Claire she loved her. Propelled by a combination of fury and desire, she summoned every ounce of strength she could muster and hurled her body into Warren's again. She saw the gun fly through the air at the same time she heard Claire's voice shouting her name. When she looked up, Claire was standing over Warren who lay sprawled on the ground, her gun pointed at his chest.

"Riley, are you okay? Can you move farther away from him?"

She answered with a grunt and rolled away, keeping Claire and Warren in her sight.

"Claire, are you okay?"

Riley turned her head for a second, long enough to see Nick running toward them. She watched him take Claire's place, and a second later, Claire dropped to her side and started working to free her. She forced the words to come. "You came," she whispered.

"Of course, I did," Claire said, tugging at the rope that held her hands. When they were free, she pressed them gently to her face. "I was scared I'd be too late."

"It's okay."

"No. There are things I want to say. Important things." Claire glanced over at Warren, and Riley followed her gaze. Nick still had him at gunpoint, but she understood they needed to get him secured so they would all be safe.

"Go. Tell me later." Claire started to get up, but Riley motioned for her to come close. When Claire's ear was next to her mouth, she whispered the one thing she wanted Claire to know no matter what happened with Warren or her father or her own future. "Love you."

Claire leaned back so Riley could see her face. She wore a broad smile and tears gathered in the corner of her eyes. "Love you, too."

CHAPTER TWENTY-ONE

Three weeks later

Riley stood in the center of the gallery, completely overwhelmed at the sight of her work covering the walls. Every aspect of the installation showcased the city exactly the way she saw it, and she hoped whoever came tonight would feel immersed in the glory of the sights most Dallasites took for granted.

"Are you excited?"

Riley reached out and clasped Claire's hand. "Yes. And a little scared. What if no one comes?"

"I bet every artist is scared no one will show up to their debut, but Lacy's done a bunch of these and she's got enough wine and snacks in the back for half the city. I have a feeling you're going to be surprised." Claire motioned behind her. "See, Cheryl and Nick are here. I'll have to warn Lacy to put out more food."

"Very funny, Ms. Squad Commander," Nick said. "I guess now that you've been promoted, my hunger is no longer your problem. Well, Cheryl's already picked out a couple of pieces she intends to take home, so I think I've earned my snacks tonight."

"Don't listen to her," Riley said. She started to ask Cheryl which pieces she had her eye on, when a familiar voice spoke first.

"Are we early?"

Riley turned to face her father. He was standing with her mother a couple of feet away, his expression tentative, and she motioned for them to join her and Claire. She'd made a concerted effort to reconnect with her father since his exoneration and Warren's arrest, and during the time they'd spent together, she gained a new respect for what he'd gone through during his time in prison and his decision to use some of the restitution he'd received to fund a paid intern for the local office of the Innocence Project. Riley liked the idea of having a father again even if they were still navigating what exactly that meant for the two of them. He was still a bit cautious around Claire, but she'd made it clear to both her parents, Claire was one of the good cops and she was in her life to stay.

If it wasn't for Claire, she might be dead right now, and she shuddered when she thought about how close Warren Spencer had been to taking her life. She'd been stunned to learn the sweet, older gentleman who she'd thought had shared her love of art was really a bitter, angry victim who'd spent years dwelling on taking revenge against her father who he was certain had killed his daughter. He was so fixated he still refused to accept the recent DNA results that proved Milo Shaw was the real killer, but Claire assured her he'd have plenty of time to come to terms with the truth while he was in prison.

"No, you're right on time," Riley said to her father. She pointed across the room at Lacy who was headed toward them.

"Are you ready?" Lacy asked.

Riley nodded at the loaded question and watched Lacy walk to the door and begin welcoming the guests. Mixed in with the flood of strangers were a few dear, familiar faces: Buster and Natalie, Jensen with a cute guy on his arm who she was sure he'd introduce to her later, and Morgan and Parker. From her work on the walls to the friends who'd gathered to support her art to the wonderful woman on her arm, her life was full. She leaned in close to Claire and whispered, "I'm ready for anything with you by my side."

Claire looked lovingly into her eyes. "And that's exactly where I'm going to stay. For the rest of my life."

THE END

About the Author

Carsen Taite's goal as an author is to spin tales with plot lines as interesting as the cases she encountered in her career as a criminal defense lawyer. She is the award-winning author of over twenty novels of romance and romantic intrigue, including the Luca Bennett Bounty Hunter series, the Lone Star Law series, and the Legal Affairs romances.

Books Available from Bold Strokes Books

All the Paths to You by Morgan Lee Miller. High school sweethearts Quinn Hughes and Kennedy Reed reconnect five years after they break up and realize that their chemistry is all but over. (978-1-63555-662-9)

Arrested Pleasures by Nanisi Barrett D'Arnuck. When charged with a crime she didn't commit Katherine Lowe faces the question: Which is harder, going to prison or falling in love? (978-1-63555-684-1)

Bonded Love by Renee Roman. Carpenter Blaze Carter suffers an injury that shatters her dreams, and ER nurse Trinity Greene hopes to show her that sometimes hope is worth fighting for. (978-1-63555-530-1)

Convergence by Jane C. Esther. With life as they know it on the line, can Aerin McLeary and Olivia Ando's love survive an otherworldly threat to humankind? (978-1-63555-488-5)

Coyote Blues by Karen F. Williams. Riley Dawson, psychotherapist and shape-shifter, has her world turned upside down when Fiona Bell, her one true love, returns. (978-1-63555-558-5)

Drawn by Carsen Taite. Will the clues lead Detective Claire Hanlon to the killer terrorizing Dallas, or will she merely lose her heart to person of interest, urban artist Riley Flynn? (978-1-63555-644-5)

Every Summer Day by Lee Patton. Meant to celebrate every summer day, Luke's journal instead chronicles a love affair as fast-moving and possibly as fatal as his brother's brain tumor. (978-1-63555-706-0)

Lucky by Kris Bryant. Was Serena Evans's luck really about winning the lottery, or is she about to get even luckier in love? (978-1-63555-510-3)

The Last Days of Autumn by Donna K. Ford. Autumn and Caroline question the fairness of life, the cruelty of loss, and what it means to love as they navigate the complicated minefield of relationships, grief, and life-altering illness. (978-1-63555-672-8)

Three Alarm Response by Erin Dutton. In the midst of tragedy, can these first responders find love and healing? Three stories of courage, bravery, and passion. (978-1-63555-592-9)

Veterinary Partner by Nancy Wheelton. Callie and Lauren are determined to keep their hearts safe but find that taking a chance on love is the safest option of all. (978-1-63555-666-7)

Everyday People by Louis Barr. When film star Diana Danning hires private eye Clint Steele to find her son, Clint turns to his former West Point barracks mate, and ex-buddy with benefits, Mars Hauser to lend his cyber espionage and digital black ops skills to the case. (978-1-63555-698-8)

Forging a Desire Line by Mary P. Burns. When Charley's ex-wife, Tricia, is diagnosed with inoperable cancer, the private duty nurse Tricia hires turns out to be the handsome and aloof Joanna, who ignites something inside Charley she isn't ready to face. (978-1-63555-665-0)

Love on the Night Shift by Radclyffe. Between ruling the night shift in the ER at the Rivers and raising her teenage daughter, Blaise Richilieu has all the drama she needs in her life, until a dashing young attending appears on the scene and relentlessly pursues her. (978-1-63555-668-1)

Olivia's Awakening by Ronica Black. When the daring and dangerously gorgeous Eve Monroe is hired to get Olivia Savage into shape, a fierce passion ignites, causing both to question everything they've ever known about love. (978-1-63555-613-1)

The Duchess and the Dreamer by Jenny Frame. Clementine Fitzroy has lost her faith and love of life. Can dreamer Evan Fox make her believe in life and dream again? (978-1-63555-601-8)

The Road Home by Erin Zak. Hollywood actress Gwendolyn Carter is about to discover that losing someone you love sometimes means gaining someone to fall for. (978-1-63555-633-9)

Waiting for You by Elle Spencer. When passionate past-life lovers meet again in the present day, one remembers it vividly and the other isn't so sure. (978-1-63555-635-3)

While My Heart Beats by Erin McKenzie. Can a love born amidst the horrors of the Great War survive? (978-1-63555-589-9)

Face the Music by Ali Vali. Sweet music is the last thing that happens when Nashville music producer Mason Liner, and daughter of country royalty Victoria Roddy are thrown together in an effort to save country star Sophie Roddy's career. (978-1-63555-532-5)

Flavor of the Month by Georgia Beers. What happens when baker Charlie and chef Emma realize their differing paths have led them right back to each other? (978-1-63555-616-2)

Mending Fences by Angie Williams. Rancher Bobbie Del Rey and veterinarian Grace Hammond are about to discover if heartbreaks of the past can ever truly be mended. (978-1-63555-708-4)

Silk and Leather: Lesbian Erotica with an Edge edited by Victoria Villasenor. This collection of stories by award winning authors offers fantasies as soft as silk and tough as leather. The only question is: How far will you go to make your deepest desires come true? (978-1-63555-587-5)

The Last Place You Look by Aurora Rey. Dumped by her wife and looking for anything but love, Julia Pierce retreats to her hometown, only to rediscover high school friend Taylor Winslow, who's secretly crushed on her for years. (978-1-63555-574-5)

The Mortician's Daughter by Nan Higgins. A singer on the verge of stardom discovers she must give up her dreams to live a life in service to ghosts. (978-1-63555-594-3)

The Real Thing by Laney Webber. When passion flares between actress Virginia Green and masseuse Allison McDonald, can they be sure it's the real thing? (978-1-63555-478-6)

What the Heart Remembers Most by M. Ullrich. For college sweethearts Jax Levine and Gretchen Mills, could an accident be the second chance neither knew they wanted? (978-1-63555-401-4)

White Horse Point by Andrews & Austin. Mystery writer Taylor James finds herself falling for the mysterious woman on White Horse Point who lives alone, protecting a secret she can't share about a murderer who walks among them. (978-1-63555-695-7)

Femme Tales by Anne Shade. Six women find themselves in their own real-life fairy tales when true love finds them in the most unexpected ways. (978-1-63555-657-5)

Jellicle Girl by Stevie Mikayne. One dark summer night, Beth and Jackie go out to the canoe dock. Two years later, Beth is still carrying the weight of what happened to Jackie. (978-1-63555-691-9)

Le Berceau by Julius Eks. If only Ben could tear his heart in two, then he wouldn't have to choose between the love of his life and the most beautiful boy he has ever seen. (978-1-63555-688-9)

My Date with a Wendigo by Genevieve McCluer. Elizabeth Rosseau finds her long lost love and the secret community of fiends she's now a part of. (978-1-63555-679-7)

On the Run by Charlotte Greene. Even when they're cute blondes, it's stupid to pick up hitchhikers, especially when they've just broken out of prison, but doing so is about to change Gwen's life forever. (978-1-63555-682-7)

Perfect Timing by Dena Blake. The choice between love and family has never been so difficult, and Lynn's and Maggie's different visions of the future may end their romance before it's begun. (978-1-63555-466-3)

The Mail Order Bride by R Kent. When a mail order bride is thrust on Austin, he must choose between the bride he never wanted or the dream he lives for. (978-1-63555-678-0)

Through Love's Eyes by C.A. Popovich. When fate reunites Brittany Yardin and Amy Jansons, can they move beyond the pain of their past to find love? (978-1-63555-629-2)

To the Moon and Back by Melissa Brayden. Film actress Carly Daniel thinks that stage work is boring and unexciting, but when she accepts a lead role in a new play, stage manager Lauren Prescott tests both her heart and her ability to share the limelight. (978-1-63555-618-6)

Tokyo Love by Diana Jean. When Kathleen Schmitt is given the opportunity to be on the cutting edge of AI technology, she never thought a failed robotic love companion would bring her closer to her neighbor, Yuriko Velucci, and finding love in unexpected places. (978-1-63555-681-0)

Brooklyn Summer by Maggie Cummings. When opposites attract, can a summer of passion and adventure lead to a lifetime of love? (978-1-63555-578-3)

City Kitty and Country Mouse by Alyssa Linn Palmer. Pulled in two different directions, can a city kitty and country mouse fall in love and make it work? (978-1-63555-553-0)

Elimination by Jackie D. When a dangerous homegrown terrorist seeks refuge with the Russian mafia, the team will be put to the ultimate test. (978-1-63555-570-7)

In the Shadow of Darkness by Nicole Stiling. Angeline Vallencourt is a reluctant vampire who must decide what she wants more—obscurity, revenge, or the woman who makes her feel alive. (978-1-63555-624-7)

On Second Thought by C. Spencer. Madisen is falling hard for Rae. Even single life and co-parenting are beginning to click. At least, that is, until her ex-wife begins to have second thoughts. (978-1-63555-415-1)

Out of Practice by Carsen Taite. When attorney Abby Keane discovers the wedding blogger tormenting her client is the woman she had a passionate, anonymous vacation fling with, sparks and subpoenas fly. Legal Affairs: one law firm, three best friends, three chances to fall in love. (978-1-63555-359-8)

Providence by Leigh Hays. With every click of the shutter, photographer Rebekiah Kearns finds it harder and harder to keep Lindsey Blackwell in focus without getting too close. (978-1-63555-620-9)

Taking a Shot at Love by KC Richardson. When academic and athletic worlds collide, will English professor Celeste Bouchard and basketball coach Lisa Tobias ignore their attraction to achieve their professional goals? (978-1-63555-549-3)

Bold Strokes Books
Quality and Diversity in LGBTQ Literature